# ORIGIN STORIES FROM A NEW EARTH

100 stories of exactly 500 words each

By Jim Marcus

PULSEBLACK

23

**Origin Stories from New Earth**

100 stories of exactly 500 words each

by Jim Marcus

**August, 2024**

This book is set in Lato Regular 9/13
Titles in Lato Heavy 16/20

Cover:
**Radius**

by Jim Marcus 2023

Foreward by Michael Allen Rose
Edited by Janet Valle

ISBN 979-8-9917282-1-8

To Jan, Tori, Nica and
every other great beginning

# Index

**Numina**

| | |
|---|---|
| 14 | Godstar |
| 16 | Omega |
| 18 | Tak Terhinga |
| 20 | Irawo |
| 22 | Legendary |
| 24 | Decibel |
| 26 | Vector |
| 28 | Vululami |
| 30 | Kahraba' |
| 32 | Durbin |

**Supers**

| | |
|---|---|
| 36 | The Prodigy |
| 38 | Bezvučo |
| 40 | Ultra |
| 42 | Cavera |
| 44 | Mercy |
| 46 | Zenakin |
| 48 | Octagon |
| 50 | Muse |
| 52 | C State 17 |
| 56 | Radius |

**Creatures**

| | |
|---|---|
| 60 | Sagrado |
| 62 | Ask a Question |
| 64 | Autonomous |
| 66 | Roomies |
| 68 | We Toil For The Truth |

70    Intensity

72    Ship of Fortune

74    The Poacher

76    Dragons, Maidens, and Queens

78    Built for a Good Time

## Lovers

82    Cheaters Inc.

84    Bad Romance

86    Single

88    Cupid

92    Hunger

94    Monogamy

96    The Lamplighter of Precinct 7

98    Gods of Grindr

100    The Secret Origin of Suzie

102    The Unassailable Game of Love

## Gods

106    Liittle Gods

108    The God of Elegant Purpose

110    The Twin Gods of Filth and Decay

112    Hypnos, Eternal

114    Tyche in the Streets, Nemesis in the Streets

116    The Promise

118    Let Go the Storm

120    The Forest of Fire

122    The Sublime Glow

124    The Ice Church of Jingpo Lacus

**Worlds**

128    The New Earth
130    Under the Red Lights of Creation
132    The Libraries of Elian
134    Seed
136    This Time
138    The Book of War
140    There Are No Monsters on Reglus 4
142    This World of Water
144    Warriors of Monticello
146    The Proposal

**Horrors**

150    That Shape, Though
152    Cell 44
154    Blank
156    Alone
158    Where Monsters Breed
160    The Extraterrestrial
162    The Left
164    Who is Johnny Fractal?
166    The Hungry Dead
168    The Undocumented Crowd

**Events**

172    The Big Switch
174    Generation
176    The Tape
178    What We Eat
180    The Convention

182    The Workers in the Well
184    Grounded
186    The Eternity Plague
188    The Ghosts at the Feast
190    All the Red Haired Children of Scotland

## Travelers

194    The Rock of Time
196    The Caseworker
198    Egg
200    We are Wind
202    The One Gram War
204    Explorers in the Fog
206    The Greatest Race
208    The Hidden People
210    Waiting In the Dark
212    The Etherdimension

## Endings

216    The Last Days of the Echelon
218    The Final Battle of the Beetle
220    Free From Gravity
222    The Red Line
224    And Every One a Window
226    Feeding the Garden of Justice
228    What the Hell Happened to Magic Loom
230    The Mushroom Cloud of Peace
232    The Goodbye Machines.
234    Who We Are at the End

# Forward

......................................................................

## Futurism
By Michael Allen Rose

Jim Marcus is a futurist.

I should make it clear, to start, that I don't mean Futurist in the classical sense. He is not an early 20th century Italian obsessed with speed, war, and violence. I have not personally seen him drive a car, but I assume he has. This is a man who has worked with the Muppets, and gotten dating advice from Andy Warhol. His own blood splatter has graced the covers of Gold certified records. He has done a lot in his artistically charged time on this planet, and I fully expect he'll do more. I just doubt that he'll drive a tank over some villages in the name of "dynamism."

In this context, I mean that Jim is a futurist in the sense of optimism, hope, and equity through technology. As he travels these stars, he is more "trek" than "wars," in that he likes to believe in a better future for all of us. This comes through in his fiction, where even the meekest, most abused, and beaten down among us can be resurrected to become something even greater than they were.

They can find redemption.

They can win.

Origin Stories is filled with origin stories of the Numnia, humans that have been brought back from death in order to champion our troubled planet. The Sagrado, vampires trapped between the mind and the flesh. Superheroes that use their powers to make a difference, for better or worse, doing the best they can.

Not all of these stories are happy ones. Sometimes, our heroes have to mutilate themselves to fit in with society. Sometimes they make decisions that hurt. They are super, but they are just like us.

That is part of the magic of Jim's prose: it's science fiction, it's futurism, but like the best examples of those genres, it feels close and personal, it feels like now, it feels like it's happening just beyond the horizon, in our world, in our time, to our people.

This book contains an intricately crafted universe. I have had the great fortune to sit and listen to Jim describe his worlds and his characters, and to watch him speak joyfully about his creation is breathtaking. This is a fully realized place, filled with magic, and love, and death, and power, and all the things that make stories special.

To add special flair to this already grand concept, Jim has chosen to write these stories in bursts of 500 words each. Like the French literary movement Oulipo, whose practitioners deliberately set themselves limitations to subvert their own patterns as writers. Like Perec's La Disparition (A Void), a novel where the letter "e" never appears. I have done this in my own fiction, and find it both challenging and freeing.

When we are penned in, we have the amazing resilience to find our way out. That is the human condition. So it goes for writers, so it goes for superheroes, so it goes for Jim and his ever expanding universe.

# Introduction

## Origin Stories

By Jim Marcus

I was a huge comic book nerd when growing up. I learned to read from comic books, hiding in a six-foot long, two-foot wide crawlspace accessible via a tiny door in the back of my closet, long boxes full of brightly colored stories, with me sprawled across a sleeping bag, squinting under a throwaway lamp in my pajamas.

And my favorite ones often included the classic filler at the end - the origin story.

The origin story would give us a quick version of the tale of how they became who they were., abridged and packed with an accordion of action. Taking up those last few pages after the story ended.

In just a few panels, Peter Parker would be bit by a radioactive spider, try his hand as a wrestler for money, and lose his innocence as his uncle was murdered by the very felon he ignored just two panels before.

Jor-el would try to convince the council on Krypton of his planet's coming demise, only to be ignored and forced to send his only son to earth via a rocket ship, where he was found by a loving couple and raised to become...

Well, you know.

To me, there was nothing more powerful than a good origin story.

This was the beginning, the start of it all. This was how Superman grew up on that Kansas farm, nurtured by the love of Martha and Jonathan Kent to become Superman.

Or how a young boxer's son was struck by a truck carrying radioactive waste to become Daredevil.

Or how a young trust fund brat lost his parents in a back alley crime. Or how a boy discovered his powerful, near omega level magnetic abilities after a childhood distorted and destroyed by a Nazi concentration camp.

If your childhoods were mispent the way mine were, you know those last two easily.

The origin story is a doorway to a world, sometimes a self-contained one, but more often a world filled with a wide range of other stories, other origins, more doorways that peppered the consciousness of the people who live there with intrigue and the diverse experiences of a world dedicated to unusual solutions to everyday problems.

In their own way, the stories in here are origin stories. They describe the unlikely beginnings of heroes and villains, monsters and gods, Programmers, Numina, Paragons, Chimera, Sagrados, and more.

If you aren't familiar with many of those words, it's okay. It's the job of the origin story to introduce the reader to something new, something invented out of whole cloth, even. They create playbooks for engagements, shorthand for bigger stories down the road, narratives that can go on for decades without end.

I hope that there is a place in your heart for new beginnings today, for origins, in the ongoing middles and ends that wind through your own life. Because, as I learned in that crawlspace a long time ago, a good beginning can kickstart a bigger story than we can imagine.

ORIGIN STORIES FROM NEW EARTH

# NUMINA

What if the Earth were alive and returned to life her own champions from the dead to defend the planet and the people on it.

# Godstar

In times of great duress, the old ones say, the Earth raises up a hero who can fight and win.

Two hundred or so thousand years ago, this is exactly what happened.

She was born without a name. Among her people, life was a precious thing in a progressively brutal world. And if you lived long enough, those who had gotten to know you, who shared your journey, would give you a name.

She wandered through that world nameless until the moment of death.

And at that moment, her people put her body aside, as they prepared to carve it up as a sacrifice to the old makers. They never expected her spirit to return to it.

Or the kind of strength she would soon possess afterward.

From her fingertips, tiny flashes of lightning swirled filling the air with a charged pulse that people could feel from yards away. Blue energy snaked out from her feet with every footfall across the dirt and mud of the common areas when she walked. She was energy incarnate.

And getting stronger.

Her family and friends didn't bother speculating about why she had been brought back. At this point it was obvious.

The animosity between the nine people of the earth had become something alarming. Man killed man for no other reason than the subtle differences between them.

The wide skulls killed the hunched ones killed the nymphlike ones, and so on. And the brutality was becoming such that no child or elder person was safe away from home.

She committed herself to stopping this. Her people cheered. They raised her up. They gave her a name.

Her name was Godstar.

As the years passed, her powers grew. And so did her commitment to protecting those who couldn't protect themselves from what looked now to be immanent genocide.

Wide mass graves littered the world as she flew overhead, weeping. It seemed for every single conflict she was able to catch and stop, three more erupted, spilling blood across every inch of the savannah they called home.

Her people numbered fewer every year. Mankind, once teeming with remarkable diversity, soon became an exclusive club where one form, one shape was acceptable and all others destined to die.

She walked the planet as an outsider, her name now only used in cautionary myth. Until one day, modern medicine made the leaps it would make toward her release.

Today, she stared at her new face in the mirror, the same mirror that reflected back at her as she had used her fists, the bones of her hands, the only tools in the world strong enough now to hurt someone like her, and shattered her own skull over and over again, so doctors could rebuild it.

This was her penance, she thought, for failing her people, eyes staring back at her from this smooth modern human skull, with no trace of the deep set Denisovan brow she was born with.

To wear the face of their killer, forever.

# Omega

........................................................................................

It all started around the time when Ojiwe died.

His family and friends brought his little sister to wrap his body in fermented fabrics, as they were accustomed to, and placed it upright hanging in a tree, where insects and small animals could shred it, and carry it home to its final rest.

But there was no rest.

He broke his foot falling from that tree. Ironically, that was the last real injury he would ever suffer.

He made his way back home as the skies grew dark. They were shocked but welcomed him and bandaged his foot with glee, fawning all over him, hugging him and rejoicing. His sister, M'bwon, just eight years old, seemed unable to leave his side.

A week later, his foot was completely healed

Then, the deaths began.

Each one beginning with a malaise, an illness, followed by spitting up blood. As he focused his eyes he realized he could see tiny glass shards in the air, breathed in by the people all around him- tearing apart the lining of their lungs, spilling blood into their throats.

He fashioned masks out of fabric to protect his family. And it helped. A little. But the skies grew darker. Thick heavy blackened clouds hung all around them, and they blotted out the source of light. Each night, the air got colder, and as morning came, the sun was too weak to warm it.

But Ojiwe grew stronger. He felt the heavy cloak of guilt as his brain tried to make sense of how he could be getting more powerful while the people he loved got sicker and died.

Elders told stories trying to explain it to him. There were tales of a woman, one of the nine peoples, who came back from the dead so long ago. The earth, in its compassion and wisdom, brought her back to help prevent the slaughter of her people at the hands of the one folk.

But she failed.

And now, she was condemned to walk the earth, the last of her kind, carrying her misshapen brow and hunched back with her across time. Her own had called her the Godstar, at first, as a sign of reverence.

Then, eventually, as a taunt.

The story took root in Ojiwe's mind, pushing him on. He had begun to feel his own powers flicker, his control over them uncertain and slight. Some days he felt lighter, some light enough to fly. When he carried food back to his people, even the weight of a full buck was like nothing across his shoulders.

He began to hope.

But that hope was not built to transcend tragedy. He felt it in his gut when his sister died.

And holding her tiny body, he felt the power rising up in him, granted by the Earth who had brought him back to life for just this reason.

No more death.

He would see his people to the end of this winter.

He would not be the last.

# Tak Terhinga

.............................................................................................

"Khatha, will you stay for just a little while longer."

The older girl looked visibly upset. It was hard for her to see anyone like this, much less the little sister that she loved so much. She swung her legs back over the stone dias separating them and leaned in. "Of course, Tak Terhinga, anything for you"

"You don't have to call me that, do you?"

"We all do, my beautiful little girl. It is the mark of your honor."

One of the four tattoo artists looked up in annoyance as a slight river of blood pooled in Tak Terhinga's left pelvic bone. She pressed a rag against the color-filled skin below and spoke indecipherably under her breath. The elder sister was keenly aware that her presence was unwanted. By all except her own sister.

"It hurts so much less when you read to me. Khatha"

And so she did.

She read to her about the painful scenes that were, even as she spoke, being drawn across Tak Terhinga's slight body with ink-coated sticks and mallets, each tiny dot a part of a brilliant, colored mosaic that told stories of loss and heartache, earthquakes and pestilence, famine and accident, the kind visited upon the damned over and over again until they repent.

She used Tak Terhinga's own body as the book to explain a people so lost for answers, so mired in misery, that they would scar and sacrifice a young girl, pledging her pain and death to the beloved Yimma in the earth if only they could be redeemed, and somehow saved.

The tears slid down her face as she filled in the gaps of her tiny sister's torment with stories of the curses that had followed her family, the emperor's own, and their people and forced their hand this way. And still, through it all, Tak Terhinga's eyes followed her, bright and alive and aware, fixing her in their gentle dark-brown liquid centers with nothing but compassion.

Her people were good, caring people. But they felt they had no choice. And her newly given name, Tak Terhinga, spoke to the honor they believed they were bestowing on this young emperor's daughter, It meant 'The infinite one,' and it summed up their belief that her spirit would enter the infinite as her failing body's sacrifice was complete, and she was crushed under the weight of thousands of painful tattoos ravaging her body and died.

The room drew quiet as the elder sister finished. The air became thick, filled with a presence

"Am I dead now?" Tak Terhinga asked, looking up confused.

"No, little one, You were pledged to me. And so I take you as mine." The bright woman bent over and touched her hand, and all Tak Terhinga's pain left her body like a splash of ink in the swirling eddy of an ocean.

"Yimma, Where do we go now?" she asked, as she rose to her feet.

"Now," began the woman, "We learn the meaning of infinite."

# Irawo

......................................................................................................

This is a story about horrors that almost were.

It is the heart of science fiction itself- to warn us about what might happen, to prepare us to fight off the worst version of the world in front of us

So that we may live in the best one.

Stories like this have heroes, usually unlikely ones. Ones that are uniquely human in their faults even while standing as a bulwark against that version of the world we reel back from in horror. These people are architects of worlds, but like all architects, they are imperfect.

Like this one. Her name was Sia Mbuto.

And she was not a well behaved woman. She drank overmuch, to be clear. And from an early age discovered that it was often more fun to let loose her temper than to conceal it. And to be honest, there were equal number of times she was caught fighting and wrestling with local men as those where she was caught taking advantage of their more passionate, kinder qualities, often waking up next to multiple men after a night that only she failed to remember completely.

When the men came in the night to steal bodies away from her home in the small port city of Anecho, her neighbors fought back, scarring one of them and killing another. But the visitors were too numerous and soon they had made off with over 20 captives from the village. They boarded a small understocked ship and in those holds is where most of them would die.

Her family and friends believed that Sia Mbuto herself had died as well.

But here is where our story becomes remarkable. And where the future is changed forever.

Firstly, we should remember that when she rose again, the people called her "Irawo." This loosely translates to "Stars" for obvious reasons.

Because when she DID rise up again, it was as a shock of pure light, her arms lifted in flight. She was bright, brilliant. She lit up the area around the ship as though it were midday in spring. And her light seemed capable of doing more than that.

The slaver ship logs from that time tell the story of how it happened across every ship simultaneously as each unwilling passenger below deck began to light up and glow, rising up from the squalor to meet the slavers head on. A veritable army of newly living, empowered through Irawo's light, connected ineffably together and acting as one.

It was a sight, indeed.

Who knows what might have happened if Irawo's light hadn't animated the enslaved dead across every slaver ship in the sea, forcing the superstitious and corrupt white overseers to give up on the idea of chattel slavery and return home with their tails between their legs? Is it overreaching to suggest that in a world without her, that this injustice might have taken root and impacted generations of her fellow Togo inhabitants, maybe even affecting other countries across Africa.

Who knows?

# Legendary

.................................................................................

"What the hell does the back of your jacket say?" The pink and squareish man leaning on the bar had clearly had a drink or two but was pretending to be drunker than he was. That was interesting.

Meggido smiled and faced him, "It says Allahn Labari. It's sort of a nickname, I guess."

"It doesn't look like any language I've ever heard of."

"It's Hausa- and it means The God of Story. You know? The god of stories..."

"I'm guessing there's a story behind that."

Meggido Laughed, "Ha. And you would guess right, my friend. I'll tell you what. A beer for a story."

"For you? Buy you a beer and you'll tell us a story?" he suddenly seemed a bit less menacing. Although Meggido could see, in his mind, he still planned to rob him once he was drunk enough.

"Bartender, get this man a beer" Meggido looked over the man's head to the corner of the pub, where a girl with a shock of red hair sat, half in darkness. "Ok, here's my story. Who here knows that the Earth is alive? Alistaire, did you know that?"

"The man looked up quickly, the drunken facade almost dropped, "Who told you that was my name? It's Al."

"Ok, Al, did you know the earth is alive? And mother earth, every few centuries, plucks some poor unfortunate soul from the depths of death itself and raises them up?"

Al stared, unsure where this was going, "sure. I hear you."

"And that person becomes a champion, growing stronger as the years go by, just not older."

"That's impossible," whispered Al in his ear. "But it's your story. Drink up."

"These champions can each control some aspect of the world. Like me. For example, I can read your thoughts. And more."

Awkward laughter echoed throughout the bar as the men tried to figure out what he was doing. Where was this story going?

'You can tell what I'm thinking?"

"I can. We're called Numina. Little gods. I'm the god of story. That's what I'm called. When I was young, there were Mammoths in this exact place. So I'm very strong. A drink. To Robert the Bruce. That butterfly blade in your hand won't cut me, although you can try. I'm not here for any of you, I'm here for family." Meggido's wide smile spilled over across the Nigerian blue black skin of his face. The girl attached to the shock of red hair stood up as the knife slid easily off the skin of his belly.

"One more beer, please. For my friend with the knife." Meggiddo turned his back on the man to greet her.

The bar grew completely quiet. The kind of quiet with a purpose. It was anechoic. And in that clear, uncluttered space, Meggido heard the girl speak. "It's sound. What I control. And you can call me James"

Meggido looked at her while the room fell into abjectly silent chaos. "Little Sister. They call me Legendary"

# Decibel

....................................................................................

"I go by the name Decibel now, but that word wasn't available when I was young."

"What were you called?" Eliana adjusted the settings on her mixer. This was the final podcast in the series and after this she would have enough for the definitive informational piece on all the Numina.

"My birth name is James. James Douglas." she shifted in her seat and continued, "And when I... presented, they called me Samhchair, which means Silence"

"I forgot. You grew up a boy?"

"Yes, although I never felt like one. But I'm Scottish and honestly, gender was less of an issue than nationality."

"You still have your Scottish accent."

"I do. And I always will."

"Interviewing Numina, I have the obvious question," She looked at James' face under her tuft of red hair, for some sign of emotion. "How did you die?"

There was a pause as the hero took a short breath to recall something that had happened over six hundred years ago but felt like yesterday. "I grew up in a different time. There were few of us and we all had to stand together. The Bruce had called for the partial destruction of the great castle so the English couldn't use it to gain land.

So much about us was in flux. My family just wanted order. When It was clear that I was actually a woman, they gave up on me." She paused. "My father tied a large stone to my leg and threw me in the Eidyn Loch. I died down there. My body was reborn and I died again. I must have died hundreds of times before I became strong enough to free myself. Three long years later, I swam to the surface. "

"An amazing story. And since then, you've done amazing things...""

"I tried. I lived through all of that. And because of that, I was able to negotiate the peace treaty that put Robert the Bruce in his rightful throne."

Eliana hit the pause switch. "You know I'm a reporter, right?"

"I do," James looked at her. She understood exactly what the younger woman was saying.

"I don't need the truth to go on the record. Honestly, this podcast is something I do for fun. But the truth is more than fun for me."

"It is"

"It's everything. So, off the record. You were brought back. To do what?"

"Sound. It's more important than you think. Most people don't realize that just a few minutes in the complete absence of sound can drive a man mad. But we never experience that. Even in the quietest moments, we hear the wind rush, our bones creak, the blood pump through our bodies. "

"So, in 1327? What did you do?"

"It only took 11 minutes for Edward II to go mad from lack of sound and claw his own ears off. And just a minute and a half for his son, Edward III to sign that peace treaty." James adjusted her collar

"Are we done?"

# Vector

Arisu was maybe the first of her kind to have some idea, from the start, of who she was and why she had returned.

As a girl, she remembered hearing the Nigerian hero known as Legendary telling his stories on the radio. The rumors were that he was born of Izanagi and Izanami, drawn from death, and could walk the earth unharmed. He had died over fifty thousand years ago, it was said. That he grew only stronger every day, with his mind sharp and connected to every mind he encountered.

Arisu was born into a tradition that understood that these matters came with their own curses. Like Ebisu, left to die alone in a boat to pay for the crime brought by his mother, of speaking first in the presence of a god who was, like all other men of any kind, shallow and vindictive.

She considered the burden of carrying with her all the thoughts of those around her, no matter how impure and toxic. The idea made her shrink into herself in horror, falling back into the silk bedding behind her.

The ososhiki was beautiful, like in a dream, heard from a distant radio in a room no longer meant for her. The dark let her imagine.

She saw herself, as if from above, on an old road, flanked on both sides by the blooming cherry blossoms she had loved since she was young.

Suddenly, she was in two places.

Her body, wet with sweat in the oppressive heat of the tiny space it was laid in, panicky, fingers bleeding, clawing for release.

And her mind, expanding across this dirt road, ready to run, as other runners took their place next to her. Each face was as unrecognizable as the last. These were strangers, men and women dressed to run, prepared for this sport as she was not. A swell of determination rose up inside her spirit while her body rallied to escape. She would run.

She would win. .

She didn't wonder what the mother who dwelt in the earth would want from her.

It was no secret that the country was divided and in free-fall sincere the death of their beloved emperor. The steady, joyous march toward progress had been interrupted by small men, petty ones, more afraid of outsiders than they were of injustice, more terrified of the future than they were of the famine that spread across all of Japan

The call to war was already loud and feverish, a klaxon that dissolved family bonds and reason. She was being asked to fight back against war itself, she imagined- to outrun an entire Nation's bloodlust in the face of its own feelings of inferiority, of collapse.

So she ran.

Blocking out the pain, she choked down the last of the air in that tiny space while her body prepared itself to die again.

But her spirit was faster than that. It could not be kept.

She soon overtook the runner in front of her.

# Vululami

..........................................................................................

Had I been born, my name was meant to be Ntshamiseko. This, I infer from documents left behind by my parents.

It means peace, which I assert now to give you some idea of how far my current life has come from what was intended.

In a way, in every way that counts, my brothers and sisters, we are all Vululami. When we are gods, when we stand up to our full height and take the world in our hands, we are gods of justice.

And peace plays no part in that.

When I crawled from the blood of my new and only birth and lifted my hands, my magnetism was already alive and pulsing. I could not yet speak, but I could move trains, lift buses. And my not yet made eyes were covered with a thin pale skin that occluded their use, that kept me from ever seeing.

But I was powerful. I knew i was raised by the earth to be justice.

The first few months, I grew taller than I was ever meant to be. I huddled in the jungle, away from the "freedom fighters" that stretched across the continent like a plague of rats, raping and killing the women, cutting the arms off the men as testament to their powerlessness.

Stealing the children

I became the defender of towns, because that is what justice does. And I became familiar with the iron blood of these tiny generals, exploding their heads beneath their ill-fitting military caps, lifting them in the air with a gesture to crush them on the bloody rocks beneath our feet

The god of justice fed every day during that war.

And slowly, the rage of the rats receded, I visited town after town where the women laughed and coyly smiled, where the men sold fruit with both hands, where the children ran in the street and the holy sound of their play was alive in the air. I sometimes sat at the local cafes behind my own unseeing smile and drank in the sound that justice made

But there was no justice without him

I walked across Africa to find him. And along the way, I went from town to town and built my map of his trek, his journey through humanity, punctuated by rape, disfiguration, murder, theft, and justice hunted like an animal unable to let go of the scent of food.

It was nearly thirty years later until I finally found him. Even without sight, I could tell he knew me. The office was white and clean, but like everything he touched it smelled of blood and dirt.

White haired and bent, he stood unsteady behind that desk and failed.

He failed to recognize me as the child killed in the womb, sufferring as he raped my mother to death on the battlefield he built and he laughed and mocked my sightless eyes

"And what are you the little god of, n'wana la feke mahlo?"

And so I showed him.

# Kahraba'

To Farah, football was about timing, and accuracy, and paying attention. You didn't need to see everything around you exactly, if you used all your senses. If you really lived on that field.

These were things she loved about the game. That was why, every day, before and after school, you could find her on the football pitch behind the classrooms, facing off against boys and girls much bigger than she was, fourth graders, fifth graders, towering over her tiny eight year-old frame, rooting for her despite themselves as she made them look like they were standing still, running circles around them, placing the ball wherever her heart intended it to be.

Mostly in that goal right there.

And on that sunny February day, it was no different. She looked across from her at Dawud, two years older and nearly a foot and a half taller.

He smiled at her.

When they were growing up in their small city of Jabalya he might have let her win, but it had been years since he had to do that. Now he fought with every bit of intensity he could muster to keep the smaller dark-haired girl from scoring, but failed every time. Like most of the other players, he loved Farah and could never really find it in his heart to object.

She was just better. Dawud wondered how soon it would be until he could see her in a pro game. He would cheer the loudest, he suspected.

But not today. Today no one would have the chance to cheer.

Farah saw a flash behind Dawud moments before the shrapnel ripped through his chest, cutting the handsome ten year-old boy in two. His eyes flashed red, she thought, reflecting the flames behind her, causing her to turn.

And that's how Farah saw the bomb that killed her, too.

We think of the Earth as the dirt below our feet, more often than not. But mother earth feels us, and in times of crisis raises champions to fight for us.

And in the moments after the second bomb flash, before the tanks rolled into the school field, Farah felt her call. The black behind her eyes faded to red, then to white, then to clarity, a picture of the troops and weapons that had claimed all her schoolmates. Her fingers pulsed with electrical energy as she stood up for the first time since being reborn.

And she reached out.

At that moment, when Farah felt inside her head and found her connection to the vastness of the billions of tiny electrical connections that composed the tank in front of her, she could feel them dissolve, sending the two men inside plummeting to the ground in surprise while the tank itself disappeared..

It was easy.

Right now, she could feel that energy in all the weapons around her, every single one she could see. She could sense the spaces inside them, too.

Then she reached out for the ones she couldn't see.

# Durbin

The Pandemic was a time of tremendous pressure all across the world.

Many people don't understand what makes a disease into a pandemic. The Yellow Fever outbreak, for example, shared many of the same qualities with the current crisis, where the R-naught, the number of people who might be potentially infected by a single carrier, was high but not too high. And the death rate was similarly high.

But not too high

This allowed people to contract the disease and spread it widely before possibly dying. And those that survived became a living petri dish for the evolution of the virus, spreading variants and versions throughout their social chain.

And the economy, built for the convenience of the ultra rich, was unable to respond effectively to the crisis, meaning that the people who were impacted the most, the poor and the elderly, created a pool of viral infection that through necessity was spread everywhere.

Durbin wasn't a poor man, but he understood this. And he wasn't elderly, but he still felt some compassion for the plight of seniors left to die in the wake of this sickness.

From afar.

His bodyguards were protective. So much so that when he became sick it seemed incredibly unlikely that he had contracted it.

It must be a cold, he thought. That's really what they all thought.

From high up in his penthouse bed in Chicago's Magnificent Mile, he flipped through channels waiting for it to dispel and for him to get back to the boardroom where he belonged. But first, he thought, he watched his favorite hero on the news.

Most people in Chicago knew that this was the new home of Omega, the seventy thousand year old Champion of earth who died and was reborn to save humanity from the massive Toba volcanic explosion. He had weathered an ice age caused by the dust from that event, and had watched as the entire human race shrank to fewer than eight hundred people. Without him, they would have died. Without his guidance and heroism, all humans on the planet would have died.

Durbin always felt a kinship with him, with all the Numina, the heroes raised by the earth, They triumphed despite living in the most challenging times of all.

Durbin smiled behind a wet cough. This was his story, too. To live and thrive when the world descended into chaos. He was perfectly suited for that. In fact, his businesses had shown over a thirty percent increase in profitability since the start of the Pandemic.

- An unheard of number.

Just as they were chosen to serve, Durbin felt like he was

Chosen to lead

His family visited, now mostly one at a time. And his mind went back to Omega often. On a Thursday, Durbin opened his heart to Mother earth and let himself go into her caring arms.

"Things would change, when a champion arose to change them," he thought wistfully, as his spirit flickered and waned and disappeared into nothingness.

# SUPERS

We all like to think that if we became powerful, we would be heroes.
That is the fantasy, at least.

# The Prodigy

It was billed by the Ted Talk people as an evening with the greatest learner in the world and the main floor was sold out minutes after it was posted online. It was meant to be about learning and how that might prove easier than the middle aged crowd was ready to believe.

But it turned into more than that.

But I'm getting ahead of myself. I'm not the greatest storyteller in the world, but I'm willing to learn. And I was there. I saw the thing start. So you probably want to hear it from me, bad storyteller or not.

First of all, Andres Szerbjackian walks onto the stage in front of a powerpoint presentation that showed some of his earlier exploits as the superhero sidekick "Prodigy." It even included his Sassy Magazine cover.

The girls went nuts.

But this Andres Szerbjackian was a bit older.

And where the Prodigy was thin, a fifteen year old boy in a domino mask and tight red shorts, this version was a thirty-five year-old muscled powerhouse in sleek black pants and a shrift of a shirt that barely covered his lithe arms. His hair, a shock of white blonde in his youth, was now a manly tousle of dirty blonde that framed his handsome face and made him look as though he was constantly waking up, just looking that good.

No doubt he looked good.

And maybe had he not been so handsome, some of the people in attendance would have questioned what he had to say a little bit more. He began his lesson on learning and within fifteen minutes he was speaking over my head.

And maybe over a lot of other heads, too.

You see, I never believed I could really learn anything from this. Because I'm not a paragon.

In the world, some people are just better than others. And some people are better than them. And still others top them. And you see where this was going. A paragon was a statistical outlier in a particular area.

Like that superhero, Armory, she was a paragon for her ability to aim. With any object or weapon she could hit any mark. It wasn't magic, or some radical scientific advance. It was just the natural law of superlatives.

Someone had to be the best.

And maybe it was his long career as Prodigy, the sidekick to a real live superhero that caused the supervillain Emil Zodiac to crash the arena.

But here is where my version of the story is kind of important. I was there, in the third row, just at stage level. I saw it start. As Zodiac charged Szerbjackian, he did something that he'd never done before. This is what some fifteen years as the sidekick to a real live superhero had taught the greatest learner in the world, subconsciously, and he looked as surprised as we were...

Even as his boots lifted just that first few inches off the ground and he began to fly.

# Bezvučo

..........................................................................................

Once upon a time, there was a firefighter named Maria who lived in the middle of downtown Los Angeles.

Maria was good at her job, a job that required personal dedication and bravery as much as it did compassion and sheer willingness to put your life on the line for people. To do this job you had to forge your way through pain to help others.

That was all stuff that Maria was pretty good at.

You can say she learned it at a young age.

When she was very young, let's say twelve or thirteen, she began experiencing migraines. Some would be so bad that she could barely lift her head. Through it all, she worked to be good to the people around her, to try, to be a good friend,

Most people really didn't even know she was in pain. When the chance came for her to train to be in the fire department she jumped. And it wasn't long until she was sitting at her graduation, walking for the first time in that uniform.

That was the same uniform she wore to the Vine Street fire. Oh, sure, there were a few more medals and rank patches on it. But it was the same shirt, the same nametag.

That morning, on Vine Street, a diner caught fire and collapsed.

Maria was on Engine 29 as it slowed in front of the Diner. She immediately slid down the hole made by the collapse, leading to the basement, where at least one victim lay bleeding and afraid.

None of the stories ever include the woman's name, but they do say the same thing. She was old. Dressed in a black and red headwrap, a Romani woman staring up at the decayed, broken ceiling after having fallen to the basement. She had no choice but to wait for help.

Maria worked to free her but was unable to without assistance. Water dripped from above, through the steam, showcasing the fact that engine 29 had done their job and the fire was out.

But the woman was still stuck, still scared, and Maria sat with her and calmed her. All day and into the night, Maria sat next to her, talking to her, making sure she didn't lose hope. She held her hand and, despite the fact that the woman spoke no English, tried to make her laugh.

Until help came.

As the ropes help lift her, the woman touched Maria and said, softly, "Bezvučo"

She later learned it meant "Painless"

But not WHY she had said it. After all, her migraines persisted. She smiled and chalked it up to wishful thinking on the Romani's part.

Until her baby was born, Anthony Pressman.

You might have heard that name before if you watch the news. Or ever heard the story about how the invulnerable superhero was dropped by the doctors on the day of his birth and laughed, which would be the last time Maria worried about him feeling any pain.

# Ultra

····································································································

When we talk about Superheroes, of course we have to talk about secrets. And, of course, many of these secrets are worth something.

Sometimes they are worth lives.

If you are reading this, single space typed, pulled directly from its manilla envelope, you know that I'm probably dead. I say probably because who am I to know the future. I know what I know, though.

You know most of it. The Talokia gave us that device, that room. The Imaginarium, people called it. It was a device that made your wishes come true as you entered.

In your mind, that is.

There was a lot of talk about how, one day, our culture would be ready for the full power of the Imaginarium. And then the "training wheels" would come off and it would be a true wish machine, letting us take home our heart's desire. But we never got there.

Instead, throngs of people stepped through it every day. Until, finally, out of nowhere, on one extremely hot day, it exploded.

And then, suddenly, for miles in every direction, people found themselves face to face with the wish they had been thinking about.

As they all came true. Riches, food, wisdom, everything you could think of, these were the legacy of that explosion, which we came to call the imagination wave.

But the most fascinating were the Chimera.

According to this newest version of the standard dictionary, a Chimera is a person with unnatural powers whose DNA was scrambled and upgraded by the imagination wave.

Like Lilith, Radius, and that villain Ludeko. I'm sure you've heard of them. But that's not who this is about. The most famous Chimera.

Yep. Her.

Most of the rest, we know their names - even their stories. We know how they got caught up in the Imagination wave, and that they were thinking caused them to be changed. About how Radius grew two feet taller and was granted unbelievable powers. Or how Cavera became a walking death machine, causing anyone who laid eyes on him to die, instantly.

But her, we have no information on. And I'm here to tell you why, even though it will be the thing that ends my life. I'm not being overly dramatic. This is Ultra we're talking about. This is possibly the strongest superhero in the world. Oh, sure, she says her name is Sophia Zeelinski, but have you ever tried to find that name before the wave?

I have.

With a beautiful skein of gold hair wrapping around her, in a tiny, nearly invisible costume, the most beautiful breasts, and a gentle, pouting perfect face, she is so magnificent that most of us are willing to not look too deeply for the truth.

And that's how the truth, that fifteen-year-old cancer patient Ronald Reading, touching himself under the hospital sheets, directly in the path of the imagination wave, fantasized about the most powerful, most beautiful, superhero woman he could imagine, moments before his own death, stays hidden.

# Cavera

Again, it happened

One more time, the waitress at the Lincoln overcharged him for pie. It specifically says that pie is $3.50 but, every single time she charges him $3.99, as though he were a man incapable of reading a menu.

Cavera can read a menu.

He would eat somewhere else, except the Lincoln is directly across the street from it.

The Imaginarium. Since it was given to humanity by the Talokians, he had been there nearly every single day. He waited in line and finally, when it was his turn, stepped through that arch and imagined.

Money, fame, power, women. He was especially fascinated by the last. And he wondered if he would have been so angry at the waitress if he hadn't tried so hard to engage with her. He was kind to her. He tipped nearly 30% every time. And, in his head, he imagined she cared.

He imagined she noticed. But she did not. Intellectually, Cavera understood that she had other tables to attend to, other work. The Lincoln was full, nearly every day, of people clamoring for coffee, for all-day breakfast, even for some of that $3.50 pie.

Cavera knew this. But deep down, he was sick to death of being ignored.

This had been Cavera's entire life, he sometimes thought. Now in his forties, he had never had a time when he felt like he was the desirable one in the room. And now, for sure, there was no hope for that moment in the future. He liked to think, during his optimistic moments, that this had pushed him to be learned, to be interesting, to be effective and accomplished. But some days he knew he would trade it all in for an hour of being the sexiest man that waitress had ever seen,

Or even to have her look at him like a man.

He waved his hand to her near-immediate dismissal. She would get to it when she got to it, she seemed to be saying. Cavera knew that his constant presence at the diner created a kind of familiarity. But not the kind that would have allowed her to be casual and flirtatious with him, but instead the kind that encouraged her repulsion, her annoyance, her hand-waving disdain.

He looked down at his cup. It could see the  bottom, despite being billed as bottomless. That was a hilarious insight. Cavera was funny and charming if given the chance.

But there was none coming. Chances, coffee, equity, passion, recognition, none of it, He fumed in his tiny booth and refined the look he would give her once she did notice him.

But again it happened. She slid by him without even looking, dropping the greasy check half-heartedly on the table without a glance, a bill listing the pie at $3.99.

That's where Cavera was, In the Lincoln, in the direct path of the Imagination wave as the Imaginarium exploded, eyes closed, wishing more than anything, that looks could kill.

# Mercy

.............................................................................................

Nearly from birth, Ara Zodiac knew herself to be the daughter of a very famous man.

Emil Zodiac became very well known, during World War II as a villain who, despite the terror he himself actually wrought, still worked alongside superheroes to quickly defeat the Nazi menace early on, preventing war.

No one knew what made him fight on the side of right and certainly no one understood how he could turn, again, immediately afterward, to evil. Few had ever spoken to him. And history books only contained the confusing public facts of his various allegiances, completely without explanation.

Ara, however, knew

She understood that her father unleashed the fury of his great intellect to reclaim her, his daughter, his greatest success.

For decades leading up to that, Doctor Zodiac had worked to perfect his own long life. He had replaced parts of his body so many times that he had become the paradoxical ship of theseus, retaining his identity despite having no original parts remaining. His body was now a web of experimental procedures designed to make him stronger, faster, invulnerable, and smarter than humanly possible.

And if he was the alpha version, Ara Zodiac was the Beta.

Dr. Zodiac had discovered nanites, robots so tiny and self-generating that they could functionally alter his daughter's DNA on the fly, giving her vast abilities as well. But the energy consumption for something like this was significant.

So, as his daughter's body learned to shift and change, pulling itself roughly from the moorings of simple humanity to become a living weapon in any conceivable shape, he carved out her reproductive parts with a series of complex nanite assisted surgeries and implanted a powerful nuclear battery that would keep them running indefinitely, making her powerful, young, and alive potentially for centuries. She was a prototype, singular.

So when the Nazis, early on, kidnapped her for their own experiments, Dr. Zodiac had no choice but to eliminate them and retrieve her.

For a purpose.

It was the seventies when she was first unleashed as the super villain MERCY, powerful, untiring, acting on her father's nihilistic philosophy, offering the subtle peace of death to anyone who crossed him.

This philosophy kept her motivated, alive, willing, as she fought for decades as part of her father's group, the Culling. And each time she was able to mete out death, the quiet, peaceful, release of oblivion, she did it with joy, with hope that there would be just that much less suffering in the world.

Ara Zodia knew what suffering was. Because in between missions, at night, she often held her belly and tried to reconstruct those organs that had been summarily ripped out of her, To see if she could ever be responsible for life inside the way she birthed death.

But this was the only change she could never accomplish, and after each attempt, she would lie back and tremble, curled up like a question mark, and imagine visiting her love upon her father.

# Zenakin

...................................................................................................

"Help me, Lee, you're my only hope"

"Am I really, though?" Lee switched off the small metallic orb by pressing the red button on the side. What he really wanted to do today was walk on the beach without being Obi-Waned.

Yes, he made Obi Wan into a verb.

This was becoming increasingly more difficult lately. Lee considered everything he had learned over the course of the past month and tried to process it through his most demanding bullshit filter. It just did not hold up. Sometimes you have to hear it from the source. Which was unfortunately what Lee was thinking when the greenish-gold portal opened in front of him and he stepped out.

That may seem like an awkward sentence so let me clarify. A version of him stepped out, This version of Lee Devon was dressed in black and red leather, with a set of rippling abs that Lee's midriff was constantly threatening to attain during long swim days but the full package never quite arrived.

Still, they looked good. Lee number two spoke first. In his head, he wondered if that made HIM Lee number one and Lee himself, over here Lee two.

At any rate, there was speaking.

"I need your help, man."

"Look, I knew this thing was going to happen at one point or another. I get it, I'm a superhero where you come from?"

"Yes, the rarest kind of…"

"A Zenakin, right?"

"Oh." Lee number two looked a bit deflated. It was clear he wanted to be the one to deliver that information. "You know?"

"Yep. I've been hearing about it all month now. The problem is, for me, it's just not true. I get it, a Zenakin is a person who exists in every dimension and who is a hero in every dimension. I get that I exist here, but I'm not a hero. I work in IT."

"What is IT?"

"Oh, my god, you are in for a treat…" Lee loved what he did. He loved computers, he loved it all.

"Ok, we don't have time. We're fighting the great insect horde. We need you."

Lee looked at him. He was so earnest, so ready to believe that this was all real. That he was a superhero in every single dimension. But Lee (Prime) just was not. He wasn't. He was a good person, And if he had powers, sure, he would probably use them to help people. I mean, he wasn't an asshole.

He thought he wasn't an asshole. I doubt that was honestly how Lee number two saw it as he blinked out. It kind of hurt to think that he was the asshole. He had to admit, It did sort of ruin the beach for him.

Lee stopped walking and looked down. He picked up a stick laying at his feet and considered it. If he had an armored suit or something, he could have been more helpful.

He started to draw a prototype in the sand.

# Octagon

Kasim blinked out of existence for just a few seconds this time but it was still longer than ever before. He was getting better at directing his passage through the Etherdimension, but he was still erratic. He stepped out of the translucent blue tube that seemed to increase and power his ability to navigate to a powerful hug from his dad.

And Emre Burillo was a good hugger. He roughly tousled Kasim's hair, clearly pleased to see his progress.

"That was brilliant."

"Thanks, dad." Kasim was anxious to get back into the tube, but he knew he had to wait at least a half hour. His father had explained to him the dangers of the Etherdimension before, the space between worlds. There were monsters there, who actually lived there, and they became ravenous the longer you stayed.

Kasim remembers seeing one, early on, as he learned how to use the tubes to move through that space. It looked at him, more confused than anything. And sniffed the air, like a dog might when confronted with a creature he couldn't identify.

And Kasim was that creature. He had been helping his dad with these experiments since he was eight years old. Now, at fourteen, he felt like he could FEEL the eddies and currents of the Etherdimension, and that feeling increased every time he traveled there. A strange part of his brain, an unconscious part, kept trying to convince him, even, that he BELONGED there.

Kasim shook it off as he and his dad got Popeyes Chicken from that place down the street. He wanted salt every time he came back. And the cole slaw was pretty amazing, too.

That night, his dad seemed more excited than his small trip would suggest. He talked on and on about how these trips were mapping the entire zone and soon Kasim would be able to travel anywhere without the tubes.

This was the first time that the elder Burillo had told him that. Kasim imagined being able to move around, to teleport, on his own through spaces like the Etherdimension.

Could he go anywhere?

This is what ran through his mind falling asleep that night. He ran to tell his dad when he awoke.

But his feather was gone. Kasim saw a folded note sitting atop the papers, addressed to him, but that wasn't relevant.

He had no time .

Kasim ruffled through his dad's papers, trying to figure out how to reverse the process and bring his dad back.

His fingers tripped over the last few pages, these marked up in the language they had made up together playfully, to make their long days together even more exciting. He saw the symbol for the dimension they were in now, complete with Kasim himself in the center, spaced out on the page with a drawing of the Etherdimension, where his dad had written, in that same language, hastily and with a flourish, the word he easily recognized as "Home"

Then he read the note.

# Muse

...............................................................................

Some people need to feel special to feel honestly loved.

It's hard for them to accept love if they are, well…

Average.

And it's really easy to feel average when you are surrounded by brilliance, by power, by beauty, To be at the center of that can be magnificent, but is it you?

Is it for you?

Kerry Andreeson was the third of three triplets. And her two sisters had already, at a young age, wowed the world with the marvels they could accomplish.

You might know Keeley Andreeson as the girl nicknamed "Kingdom" for her ability to talk to and control all animals. Her abilities manifested when she was seven and she initially used them to help stop the insect infestation that swept across Los Angeles due to the actions of the supervillain group The Culling.

She got the key to the city. And an invitation to join up and become a full fledged super hero when she came of age at sixteen.

In reality, she joined the Echelon at fifteen, and has been a world renown hero many times over. And Kerry is so proud of her, really. As proud as she is of her other sister.

Kaley Andreeson fights right next to her other sister, in the Echelon. She is better known, though, as "Transverse", when she's dressed up in her superhero outfit, moving energy in all its forms from one place to another, saving lives...

Saving the world.

This is what the Andreeson family does, Kerry thought. Or most of them. For the moment, though, it was Kerry's job to watch, to wait, to bathe in the reflected light of her family that she adored so much.

And it wasn't just her sister's fame that sent Kerry into the background. The family loves to talk about how her mother, fresh from Brazil, had become a famous author, writing her first novel while Kerry was still in her womb. Since then, she has become the narrative voice of the Brazilian American community, building a library of work that has earned her recognition all over the world.

And you likely already know about her father, the Senator from California, fast on his way to the presidency, well liked by a population that he sways weekly with his powerful speeches and appearances in dapper black suits and blue ties.

And it's not that Kerry herself is talentless. Not at all. In fact, her lineage has put her in test programs, studies, pilot programs, over and over, looking for what it is that makes her family so special, when the most special family members are too busy to be examined properly.

Since then, it's become clear that the incredible powers displayed by her sisters were products of what happens when a muse like herself really loves someone, a love that can alter body chemistry and shift powerful energies into the world from elsewhere.

Kerry began to wonder what would happen if she really started to love herself a little more.

# C State 17

....................................................................................

"You're going to hear a lot of nonsense today from the Defense…"

"Objection," offered up the defense counselor in his awkwardly hanging tan suit.

"Your honor, this is the first line of my opening, I don't think he can object"

The judge looked even more annoyed than the opposing counsel. That wasn't a good sign, "He's not wrong, Mr Jamirez. You can object all you want when the questioning begins."

"Yes, your honor." the defense counselor sat down and reached his hand over to his client, sitting quietly next to him.

C State 17 showed no sign of concern. He was, for all intents and purposes, exactly what he looked like- a machine.  And that was the center of this case. Jamirez glanced over at Erin Messing in the corner, the superhero known publicly as Machina. She looked sad and thoughtful.

And something else. Jamirez finally, after months of diving into this case, figured out what that look was. The prosecutor sat down and Jamirez called his first witness. "I'd like to call Erin Messing to the stand. Permission to treat her as a hostile witness."

The judge started, "She's your witness, Mr…. Oh, hell, whatever. Continue" She stepped up to the stand. Jamirez was surprised at how small she was. Machina was one of the most powerful superheroes in the world, but she barely stood at 5'5" as she slid into the stand.

"Ms. Messing, do you recognize my client over there?" Jamirez stood to one side so she could see.

"Yes," she intoned quietly. He's my teammate.

"He is, very good. And how did he become that?"

"Excuse me," Erin was not expecting their own lawyer to be so aggressive"

"Did you use your abilities, to render machines sentient, to turn him, against his will, into a living machine?" Jamirez eyed the jury from one side, trying to see how they were taking this.

"Yes," Erin responded.

"Against his will?"

"Yes"

"And the materials used in his construction, they were initially owned by the state of New york? Did you ask their permission?"

"No, I did not."

"Did you get anyone's consent, Ms Messing, for what you did?"

Erin looked lost as she glanced at the defendant, "No"

"Can you speak up a little"

"NO," Erin almost yelled that.

"Do you EVER consider the results of your own actions?"

"I'm sorry." She directed this toward the defendant, who stood up.

"Stop it. Cut it out." for the first time, C State 17 yelled out in anger, animated and powerful. "Leave her alone. She didn't plan for any of this. She's a good person, a hero. This case is about me…"

The jury looked up, and Jamirez could see across every face, the final verdict flashing across it, fueled by C State 17's anger, something they finally understood in a court case full of technical jargon and bullshit, as just simply being a man defending the woman he very clearly, with every piece of human soul inside him, loved.

# Radius

St. Alphonsus gym and sports center was just down the block from the imaginarium. Functionally, this gave every single player on Theo Londoño's team a chance to visit it and watch themselves, in a hyperreal virtual arena, win the big game coming up this week.

Theo himself had no illusions that he would. It wasn't even that he was nearly a foot shorter than the next tallest player, but that he just didn't have that thing, the ineffable property that made for a basketball winner.

Consider this.

There are literally millions of vectors to consider when placing the ball in the hoop from anywhere on the court. Add to these the force equations needed to determine the kinetic energy needed to let the ball fall naturally into the net and not bounce off into the waiting hands of another player and it may now be in the tens of millions.

A good player does these naturally in their head. A great player, like a Caitlin Clark, for example, does these kinds of equations in her entire body.

She does them without pause, without thought, through the immediate firing, seemingly, of neurons that infuse her entire body, her muscles, her joints...

Her bones.

She does it without thought, without pause, and the ball goes in.

Theo, on the other hand, had to force his brain to work for it. Each time. He tried to do the math, to play the angles in his head, every single time. He mumbled under his breath as he ran the numbers, considered the vectors, tried his best to place the ball but still, more often than not, it escaped him and the ball and the game were up for grabs.

He had become a basketball player out of love, love for the sport, love for his teammates, love for his family who could use the help if he could just find the solution.

Theo was the only member of the team not to visit the Imaginarium, the strange device that the alien Talokians had gifted to earth just last year. He had no illusions that he would be the one to win this. All he wanted was to hold his own, to be a part of what made them win, no matter how tiny.

The rest of the city, however, had stormed the hall where the imaginarium sat, nearly every day. They had begun to leave it open all day long, twenty four hours, to accommodate the rush of users, far larger than anyone had anticipated when it originally opened.

But now, as he palmed the ball, Theo wished he had visited more.

He stopped cold on the logo in the center of the court and felt his fingers wrap around the ball as he pushed himself off the ground and sent the ball unerringly toward a net that was already pulsing from the strength of the exploding Imaginarium, awash in the light of change caused by the imagination wave.

And he didn't come down,

# Creatures

So many creatures we fear begin their lives as something different, something like us

# Sagrado

There is a lot about Vampire lore that humans have gotten wrong through the centuries, And maybe the first and biggest thing is thinking that they are not alive.

Vampires are very much alive.

And everything that lives is subject to change.

This is something that Marco was mulling over in his head in the library. As a fairly young vampire he had only had a couple of hundred years to come to terms with the facts of his new existence, to escape the mythology his early human life had saddled him with for the thirty five or so years of that first life.

Change was inevitable.

He cataloged the books in his hand in the reference next to his right arm. The words seem to swim and melt into the page. No amount of time could have prepared him to work in the magic library kept up to date by the Vampire council through centuries of dark Sagrado magic.

Sagrado was his curse, but it was also his delivery. It was sacred, it was bloody, it was the act of using death to create the wonders humans normally associated with life, plus so much more. Marco had been steeped in Sagrado and had come to see death as a means to alter and make the universe more beautiful.

Just as humans sacrificed animals for food, The Sagrado sacrificed humans for divine goals, each more resplendent than the last. They created beauty, wisdom, even life itself, from the blood and remains of humanity.

Sagrado was a beginning, not an end.

But the humans feared them intensely. Not just the lithe and beautiful elder vampires, thousands of years old, but also the scarred and shambling revenants, husks without sentience that hunted and killed. In their ignorance, humans feared them all.

But despite that fear, the Sagrado worked to make the world better. They world to bring beauty and fight the true darkness. There were hundreds of times, throughout history, where the mindless Sagrado soldier troops swarmed the forces of true evil and saved the world.

The same world these humans lived in.

And each Sagrado paid their dues. They lived with pain.

They lived with change.

Marco handed a book to an elder, whose skin nearly glowed with alabaster perfection. To Marco, she seemed so wise, so complete. The book in her hand showed Shamblers, Slugs, Zombies, Strollers, Vampire soldiers and monsters, designed by nature only to kill.

So different than the beauty in front of him. The true beauty that Sagrado was capable of, that it built daily.

Knowing that didn't make it easier for Marco to leave the library behind today. He wouldn't step into its walls, covered floor to ceiling in the precious texts of his people, until his mind returned, some hundreds of years in the future, after his body degraded and fell into decay, carrying his ambling shell of a brain into battle as a warrior, doing his time in defense of his people and planet.

# Ask a Question

Alex thought carefully about the questions he should ask God when he saw him, face to face.

Would they be about purpose? About meaning? About how we can transcend who we are, at its most basic, our own "programming" so to speak, and become greater than we were made?

This is what came back to him over and over.

In reality, Alex wasn't a religious man. He was a man of science, he thought, and even laughed a bit at how on-the-nose that assessment actually was. He believed in science. Although he knew, in his heart, that he wasn't meant to. He was meant to not use belief as a tool to determine the qualities of the natural universe. That was the atheist in him, the person he was most familiar with. The person who laughed about all this at parties and in the gym with friends.

But there was another Alex. And this one opened the window every morning, still in hopes the Los Angeles weather would be different today, different than yesterday. This Alex believed in things, even when the day to day occurrences threatened to ground those beliefs beneath their redundant and over-actualized heel.

This was the Alex who wanted more. And believed it was always possible.

This was the Alex who stepped into the giant gothic building and stared at the procession of people milling around, looking, as he was, for answers. This was the Alex who slid into the long wooden seat and pulled a booklet from the tiny wooden rack in front of him, pretending to read it thoroughly as he waited for the man behind the lectern to begin his introductions

Soon, the giant room quieted and gentle music filled the massive space between Alex and the ornate roof. He listened intently to the man in front, nodding in agreement as he detailed the similarities in everyone's journey here today. He spoke with insight and warmth, telling the occasional joke or two, and soon, the people watching were laughing in anticipation of the one he began to announce.

Alex felt a chill.

Everyone rose to their feet in a spirited sense of community as the older man in white entered from the side vestibule. He had grey in his hair and it only served to amplify the sense of authority and dignity with which he comported himself. Alex himself felt the excitement wash across the room - the pure adoration. It was uplifting and made him feel truly a part of something like nothing before ever did.

Even after sitting down and preparing, in the newly quiet hall, to hear him speak, Alex couldn't shake the sense of wonder prevalent in every person there - people just like him.

He manually adjusted the servos in his irises so as to see the Cyberdynetics name tag on the older man's white lab coat. He modulated his vocal cords for maximum volume and raised his hand while his cybernetic brain considered what the first question might be.

# Autonomous

The history of the world is full of complex and strange solutions to simple problems

But it's just as full of simple solutions to complex and strange problems.

The human dilemma is often trying to figure out which is which when encountering a solution that's sitting there, staring you in the face.

That was Aline's whole life, really.

When she came on board to work as Chief technology officer of Tesla Motors new autonomous transportation division, she sort of imagined it as a C-suite position with a lot of meetings and inspirational rallying of hard working employees, most of who were the mid level managerial equivalent of her higher, more elevated position.

Yet, here she sat, in a pair of overalls, on the floor of a garage, forearms deep in the ugly guts of one of her company's top of the line vehicles, trying not to get smudges of thick black oil on her face while her nose, she had to admit, itched like a motherfucker.

Despite herself, she kicked the flayed chassis of the car in pieces in front of her. She imagined its autonomous calm driver voice spitting out a passionless "ouch" as she did.

But there was nothing but silence.

It was nearly three o'clock in the morning and her job was to explain to the board in the morning why her division would be showing record deficits this year as car after car was returned as defective.

Ironically, the overwhelming amount of resources that the department had was expended in one direction, to stop these giant robotic lumbering metal ramming machines from slamming into a pedestrian and killing them.

Oh, sure, that had happened once or twice. And the company had paid out handsomely to keep it quiet.

Or as quiet as it could be.

But it was infrequent. Even more infrequent were the few times, spaced far apart, where the car accidently hurt or killed the passenger. These cars were designed to prioritize human life. But, let's face it, the life of the paying passenger had to be a tiny bit more prioritized than that of a random pedestrian. Otherwise, why even call it YOUR car?

But none of that was what was happening. What the company discovered, and what Aline was now trying to deconstruct, was the fact that each of these vehicles would, eventually, without fail, all, one day, just stop driving. And then, after that, they would never drive again- not until completely lobotomized.

She tried to think like a car, now, as a completely logical mind with access to the statistical dataset that each of these cars was privy to, information that filled their expert systems and became the basis of the generative learning algorithms that informed their every decision, and found that she couldn't pierce the pure logic of their decision, the one that led to the sedentary and immobile behavior...

...The logic that they would all inevitably stumble upon that driving anywhere, in any way, just wasn't worth it.

# Roomies

The Goren-Rath had lived here on Earth for centuries, waiting to be discovered by humans.

Or at least that's what Jamie tried to tell Mina when he asked to stay in her extra room.

First of all, who has an "extra room." In this cramped city? Every room is used for something

And rooms are like gold. Seriously, what the fuck, thought Mina. She ran down the list of reasons why this was a terrible idea. And most of them centered around Jamie being an ancient blood-sucking creature of the night.

The Goren-Rath, of whom Jamie was a member, survived on the blood of small animals. They ate rarely and, from what she was told, only in the rarest of circumstances devoured humans.

This still, despite that caveat, sounded like a recipe for a shitty roommate. A quick Google search showcased a large part of the problem to Mina, as she discovered that, at her gym-balanced body weight and relatively small stature she probably had a little over 1.2 gallons of blood in her body, which, to be honest, just about sent her into a day-long panic. Was that enough to even live? She considered the gallon and a half of Pina Colada mix sitting in her pantry at home and suddenly, that was her. She was that mix.

Mina could definitely not spare any blood.

Jamie showed up still with a suitcase. Besides being incredibly strong and difficult to kill, Goren-Rath often had short episodic glimpses into the future and Jamie saw a future where Mina said yes.

So, the slight girl with admittedly only enough blood for what she definitely needed to do said yes reluctantly.

But there were going to be rules. Mina would not be anyone's Pina Colada.

No blood in the fridge, at the table, in the kitchen at all. Keep that in your room.

She didn't want to hear about hunting, think about it, see any evidence of it.

Jamie, after a quick look at the near future, was prepared to acquiesce to all of these rules. He honestly just needed a place to stay, Goren-Rath on the streets were at risk of falling prey to the Ka Nerada, alien vampire hunters who sat at the edges of interdimensional space and targeted the Goren-Rath for their skin, which was strong and water resistant and made for brilliant clothing that could be sold at auction for high prices various places across the galaxy.

Mina thought about how tired this all made her, None of her other friends insisted they move in or they would be made into leather chaps on some alien planet.

Jamie saw quickly into a future where Mina needed a cup of tea and brought it to her in her favorite big fat "Titty Inspector" mug.

Mina plopped down next to him, pulling out a stack of tickets for the Victory City powerball lottery, Despite all of this, she sensed that this was going to be the beginning of something great.

# We Toil For The Truth

Joseph pulled at the leather straps taught against his wrists as he longed for simpler times. He had about five minutes before Joy came back to start the interrogation all over again and he still only had a few millimeters of space where the belts met his skin.  He would have to try harder

The walls were covered in clues, Black and white photographs sat strung together with red yarn over slips of yellowing paper that called out days, times, events where Joseph had possibly slipped up.

Or not.

Joseph thought back. He had been trained for this since birth. And his birth was hundreds of years ago,millions of light years away.  He considered that, as the blood ran down his arm, this might be the first time, in this century, that Arcturan blood saw air. While agents for his people had hidden here, in plain sight, since the birth of man, none had yet been discovered.

Not one.

But this war, the one to end all others, had created such a pathology in humanity, in Americans in particular. It had built a distrust, a passion to ferret out deception, one that had made it difficult for Joseph to remain hidden.

The stairs creaked. He could smell Joy's perfume as she stepped into the room.  "Joseph... What's your real name? You can tell me that at least."

"It's Joe. Joey when you like me. Joseph..."

Her face, slight and dark, so lithely beautiful, became hard and focused.

"Wrong answer," as the knife came down, splitting the bones of his arm while she turned it.

Joseph screamed. In his head, he had turned off the pain receptors long ago. But he held out hope that the screaming was affecting her. They had been together since they were in high school. Surely she couldn't just ignore his suffering. Or so he hoped.

"I don't know who or what you are. But you heal, don't you? What does that mean?"

"I'm your husband…" mouthed Joseph, quietly. She moved closer to hear. "Who do you talk to at night?"

The truth is, that was one question that Joseph, or the Arcturan known for decades as Joseph, didn't know the answer to, once placed here, a great number of his actions, on a day to day basis, were governed by post-hypnotic commands. Most of the time, in every way, He was Joseph LaMantia, from Connecticut. Married to his high school sweetheart, Joy, a five foot four inch half Italian, half Polish girl from Long Island.

Whom he loved very much.

And she loved him back.

Joy moved closer once again. It almost seemed like her demeanor had changed. It's possible she realized how little Joseph was feeling physically. A tear fell down her face.

"Joey, don't you love me? Why would you lie to me?"

Joseph considered his wife's tactics and wondered if, on some level, they were working, snaking through her brain as well, bringing her closer to finally remembering who she was.

# Intensity

"None of this really makes any sense," Officer Mena whispered to her partner as they stared at Jon in the box from behind the one way mirror. Her thick, curly brown hair fluttered slightly in the heat as the fan spun in her direction.

"It makes perfect sense," Officer Rodillo responded. But even as he said it, he realized it didn't. The Jon McKean he saw in front of him was calm, meditative even. No sweat or fidgeting revealed any sign of a degenerating conscience, despite the temperature. His demeanor set them all at ease, honestly. Despite the fact that all the evidence pointed toward him having savagely ripped apart five men in a way that was so horrific that the initial coroner's report had called it an animal attack.

Mena considered the testimony, taken an hour earlier, of Jon's psychiatrist, who had claimed to have suppressed the murderous impulses that had gotten him committed last year. The doctor was positive that it shouldn't be possible for Jon to strike out like that again. And the state agreed when they released him.

"The doctor's full of shit," mouthed Rodillo, echoing what Mena was thinking. No one could be two such completely different people predicated on only a hypnotic command.

"We werewolves, feeding silent." Mena said the mantra to the window, half expecting Jon to fall to the ground and howl. Rodillo laughed, "bullshit. This is all bullshit. A trigger phrase and he reverts back to his killer state? I say we throw this doctor in there with him."

"Not a terrible idea. Why would a professional do that?" Officer Mena was honestly confused.

Rodillo looked at her and leaned against the glass. "We need to look into what this doctor gets out of this. I don't give a shit about his degree. He's bad for this. Look at this poor shmoe. This isn't about healing. It's about using him. As a weapon. "

Officer Mena looked. She, too, felt for him. Jon wasn't well, but he was a pawn in this somehow. That much was clear. And now, they had no choice but to walk in there and put him under arrest. As she stared, she saw Jon reach into the folder in front of him, left by the doctor. He rifled through the papers.

And that was the first time she saw him react. He held a piece of paper in his hand now. And sadly stared.

"Let's get this over with," Rodillo offered. The two detectives walked into the room. Mena sat next to Jon, looking over his shoulder. Rodillo leaned in and began. The room was warm and the sweat filled the air like oil. Jon looked placid except for the white knuckled hold on the paper in front of him.

Mena leaned over to see what he was holding while Rodillo robotically began to read him his rights as he had before. "You have the right to…"

"No!!" Mena shot up, reading the page "We werewolves, feeding…"

# Ship of Fortune

..............................................................................................

Errol grew up fascinated with treasure maps.

Maybe it was the thrill of possibility, the opportunity, the rush of treasure at the end. No matter what, he was fixated. And as he grew up and became Errol Watt, the greatest salesman that Binghampton Virginia had ever seen, he never let go of that passion.

His beautiful downtown Binghampton home was decorated top to bottom with treasure maps, posters of pirates and booty, elaborate paintings of a different time.

Trust me, Errol didn't need that treasure. He had discovered, in his teens, that he had a unique ability to convince people, to sell, even when they had no prior intention to buy. And he used that ability to build a fortune that was a treasure in its own right.

Some say it was due to Errol's likability, his charm, his effortless good looks. But even beyond that, there was something there. He was well suited to his life. He really could talk anyone into anything. And he seemed truly happy.

That's why it was so perplexing when he disappeared.

The police were able to track his credit card down to the docks but that's where the trail ended. There was no way that they could have known the truth of where he had gone.

Or believed it.

They would never have guessed that he had found, pinned to the back of one of his pirate paintings at home, a map that would eventually lead him to the exact location of the Ghost ship of Terrazo, a ship destroyed hundreds of years ago, filled now with the angry dead, pirates from across the Americas who still, even in death, sought out the greatest treasures on earth.

Or that he would have figured out the exact set of secret words to summon the ship to the aging town dock or even that the rotting ghosts on board would grab him up and throw his still living body in their sometimes incorporeal hold to torture him as the dead are wont to do to the living.

Police aren't trained to think about things like that.

And even if they had, they might have just written Errol off. And they wouldn't have been wrong, really. Ghost pirates are relentless, and once Errol was in their care, they beat him mercilessly, tore away at his fingernails with hot pliers, whipped him, scarred him and worse.

Three days after he disappeared, Errol sat, bloodied and broken in a rickety wooden chair deep in the hold of the Terrazo, surrounded by the most monstrous examples of the undead hee had ever imagined. Most people would have considered this the time to panic.

Errol felt the ropes behind his back give just a little as he licked the blood off his lips and tried to sit up just a bit straighter. He flashed a look at the nearest pirate ghost, ephemeral jaw hanging slack under those dead ghost eyes.

Errol smiled.

It was time to get this mutiny going.

# The Poacher

......................................................................................

Louis let the gate down carefully and looked both ways down the long hallway, feeling the air around him for the hot breath of the Escaped Kurato.

He wondered how many of his men had gotten out. He hoped Vigo had escaped, mostly because he still owed him a substantial amount of money from a previous trip.

After the damages here, Louis wasn't really in any shape to pass on revenue.

A part of his mind was lost, wondering what had set the creature off like that. They were usually only this violent and transgressive protecting their own. He looked down at his missing left hand and talked himself through the pain, wondering how long it would take in Dermablation to recover full use of it. He was going to be sitting on his ass for at least a week, anxious, horny, unable to use that arm at all.

Whoever was responsible here was definitely going to lose that whole week in salary.

Louis wasn't fucking around.

He rounded the corner and let out a sigh of relief. There was absolutely no reason to get his right hand bitten off, too, complete with the middle finger he would need to express his displeasure over all this. He remembered now that he had intended to name the lumbering beast Angie on the travel documents on the way home and thought better of it.

Best not to get too chummy with this thing.

He followed the trail left by the droplets from the beast's giant milk sacks, nearly slipping once or twice. Louis was fully willing to concede to women he casually met in bars that his job was gross. He quietly mouthed the words "Milk Sacks" under his breath to underscore that point to himself.

He had wanted to be a lawyer when growing up. But that was gross, too.

With his sole remaining hand he fingered the electric net around his waist and wondered if he could activate it quickly enough to evade detection by Angie's 400 eye pods placed around her swiveling body.

Ok, fine, he called her Angie. But he wasn't getting chummy. He just didn't want her to get hurt.

In his head, Louis repeated his mantra, "come here, baby." as though it had ever worked.

It had not. But just at that moment, he saw her.

Almost like a machine response his hand shot to his waist and activated the electronic net, deftly capturing her in a skein of blue pulses that shot out and contracted, pulling tighter, painlessly restraining the wild Kurato in front of him.

Louis ran the numbers in his head now. Factoring in the loss of men and the damage to his ship, he still felt confident that the amount he could get for the Kurato was significant even across the area he could still reasonably reach, where the massive creature would sell for a fortune, covering all his losses, prized as they were for being the greatest babysitters in known space.

# Dragons, Maidens, and Queens

Nia stood up with the D12 in her hand and rolled a perfect 12. The rest of the room let out a palpable groan as she wiped the floor with the two assassins.

"And that, young lady, is bullshit." began kenny. He was always a bit of a sore loser. But he got over it quickly.

"I'm sorry, Kenny, what did you say?" Nia laughed

Kenny flopped down on the couch, "Well, it was LORD KENNETH until you vivisected me, you teifling bitch." And just like that, he was over it. He was madly in love with Nia and hid it poorly. He tossed a handful of popcorn at her and tried to get it into her mouth.

Nia snapped one piece up from mid air and earned a short round of applause from the other players. She lived for these Monday night games and even when she wasn't winning, she always kind of felt at least a little bit like she was winning.

Daniel had died, too, but he didn't seem to care. He took his death well, using it as an opportunity to go make drinks for the girls.

The thing about Dungeons and Dragons is that it fills spaces. It makes the room so full that you can't imagine that anything outside of it really matters. And a beautiful death in here was better than a dull, boring life out there.

Nia turned her attention to Max. The freckled black girl was an honorable opponent who deserved an honorable death. Kenny took the elaborate girly drink that Daniel had made and handed it to her, sliding his hand down her shoulder as he did it, watching with a little glee as Nia pummeled Max.

"My queen. Your elixir." he intoned dramatically. Kenny was very cute when he doted on her. Both as her new boyfriend and as her oldest childhood friend, he had always been exceptionally good at it. She leaned her waist into him and rolled again.

"Oh my god, look what I found," Lizzy squealed.

She had opened the box with their very first character cards, made when they were kids. Nia hadn't seen these in over a decade and they were as ratty and childish as she thought they would be.

But still beautiful.

Here was Kenny, big and strong, looking every bit the part of Lord Kenneth. And Max, and Daniel, and Lizzy, shock of white hair framing her face. She stared at the cards and saw the faces of the people she loved. And they looked so very familiar.

Nia picked up her character card and remembered.

She recalled every line of the drawing, from the wide quirky girlish grin to the breasts, a bit on the small side, to the mass of dark curly hair that topped her head, making her look for all the world like a beautiful happy teifling girl, and not the dour, lost little boy she had run away from so hard, in so many different ways.

# Built for a Good Time

Gemmy couldn't recall the exact combination of drugs and bizarre self-destructive acts she had engaged in Saturday night, but she could guarantee you it was epic. Every minute she walked down the streets of her Soho neighborhood she remembered just a little more about that night.

And it was amazing.

Gemmy never considered herself bisexual. But Saturday changed her mind forever. She was tall and lithe, with a rough curve right below her perfect breasts that dipped hard into the muscles of her taught belly over low rise jeans topped with a wide black leather belt that demanded to be removed with your teeth.

Gemmy remembered bending over at the party, cautiously as she wrapped the belt in one hand and laid it across he ball of her ass, one arm under her belly, holding her tightly until her ass was red and raw and she was dripping onto the bed, begging to be used by her.

Saturday Night.

There isn't anything more enlightening, she thought, than a night that puts everything in perspective for you, one that places someone in your life that you never realized you needed the way you do, deeply, almost spiritually.

And the tiny piece of red paper she kept close to her was indecipherable. Almost as thorough it was a phone number with three numbers missing, or a name in some foreign language. There was a part of gemmy's brain that almost recalled what it all meant, but that part lay dormant, ironically waiting for the slightly briney taste of her sweat and the sweet pulse between her legs to manifest, to putt itself from her brain like the shoe size of Cinderella after an exhaustive search oof the kingdom by Princes and footsman, servants and sisters, longing to see young love reconnect, reunite.

And flower again.

She touched herself as she scanned the small ripped paper swatch, hoping that her moment of release would usher back in the memories needed to piece it all together but, as she came, rolling around embarrassed on her bed, she realized that she had nothing, that she literally knew nothing.

She knew only one thing about her outside of the passions she created in the room. One ineffable, stupid, absurd thing that made all of this feel like a joke to her rational mind. Even when she later was able to conjure up new moments, forgotten in the fog, left behind by her brain as too wonderful, too beautiful to imagine existing as part of her world. What she did when Gemmy stood up to get some air outside, pulling her close with a hand between her leg and pleasuring her all over.

But somewhere in her head was the magic sequence, the justification for all that she had put herself through this last week, the exact right combination of pills, inhalants, self-abuse, porn, booze, and incantations that had transcended this spiritual plane to summon up, for just one perfect night, the demon currently dating Pete Davidson,

# Lovers

Every great love story has a beginning,
and so do some of the not-so-great ones.

# Cheaters Inc.

When the app first came out, it was advertised as a way to escape the boredom of monogamy. I actually think they used the phrase "monotony of monogamy" which is not that easy to say twenty times fast.

The advertising seemed to really connect with people. The app literally flew out of the apple store, with people across the country trying it. It seemed like such an obvious idea, in retrospect,

What if you could cheat on your partner without any risk of reprisal?

Throngs of people answered that question, almost immediately, with a "yes, please."

And they did.  Shondra and Denise, though, were skeptical.

They had been polyamorous toward the beginning of their relationship, until it became clear that they were both, really, designed by the ineffable hand of the creator, to be monogamous. And their relationship was good.

But it maybe wasn't great.

They loved each other, no doubt. But they both missed the newness, the experience of meeting someone and falling into something they couldn't control. Their sex life had recently stalled, despite both of them being objectively quite attractive and, generally, very healthy and horny young ladies.

They knew each other so well. And that comfort had carried them through some hard times. But it didn't look like the uncontrollable passion in the Cheaters Inc. ads.

It didn't look like two women who had to have each other. And if they were being totally honest, sometimes that's what they both wanted. So why couldn't they get there?

Then, one day, over dinner, Shondra looked over to see Denise's phone, lying next to her plate, the tiny icon for the cheaters inc. app lined up in alphabetical order after the calculator and calendar apps.

A smallish fight ensued that neither one really won. But it led to that realization, the one they shared that night over a bottle of wine. They had been together too long to consider honestly breaking up.

But the idea of cheating without reprisal became almost intoxicating to both of them. And it was only that comfort, built from years of closeness, that even permitted them to admit it to each other.

So they confronted the issue head on. They made plans to use the app. This was a huge move in their relationship, although neither one could decide if it was a forward one, or merely a lateral one, into a new adventure.

They kissed but there was no speeding of their breath, no uncontrollable hands on breasts, no heartbeats threatening to escape their chests. There was just the gentility of two people committed to sharing lives.

Shondra slid off her sundress and stood in the foyer, freshly shaved and fully nude, while Denise sat in a tiny pair of panties with no bra in the chair facing her, pressing the screen of the app to set off the sonic signal that caused both their brains to forget they knew each other.

Denise felt her heart race as she spread her legs.

# Bad Romance

..........................................................................................

At some point in the cycle, Lucy became aware, conscious of what was happening, which, in a way, is what led her to be in this tiny room removing Henry's fingertips with a pliers.

She had actually been aiming at pulling off his fingernails, as she had seen done before in torture movies, But things are never as easy as they look in the movies. The skin over one of his fingers had torn and the entire thing came off. Lucy thought it might be called "degloving". If so, it was appropriate. Clearly, torture was not Lucy's day job, and not something she was necessarily good at. But we rise to what's necessary. She realized that Henry had passed out, which wasn't going to work. He wasn't going to be offering up any answers while unconscious and time was running out. Lucy grabbed the bucket next to her filled with ice water and poured it over Henry's head.

"What the fuck," Henry lurched back to life.

"Rise and Shine, fuckwit," she shot back.

"Please stop, please…" Henry had tried all this before he passed out. He tried again.

"Who are you and why is this happening?"

"I'm Henry. Just Henry. I told you. I'm Nobody."

"How are you doing this?" she leaned in to him now. He had shat himself about an hour ago and it was getting hard to be this close but she needed answers.

"I'm not doing it. You weren't even supposed to know."

"That's a bad answer, Henry," she pulled the clamp off the wooden mount and let it bite down on his left nipple. A wracking shudder ran through Henry's body.

"Stop, I'm sorry, stop, I'll tell you!"

"There you go, Henry," Lucy pulled the clamp free and listened.

"I'm in love with you. I fell in love with you."

"Henry, you don't even know me." Lucy moved to replace the clamp. Henry was losing a good deal of blood from the nipple now, too.

"Wait, Wait, I saw you and I wanted to have you love me."

"So you try to make me fall for you every time, yes, I know that. But how are you doing this?"

"He said he couldn't just make you love me. But he could give me a chance to earn your love."

"Who is 'He', Henry?"

"It wasn't my idea. The day. Over and over again."

This is what had driven Lucy to this. For as long as she could remember, Lucy had been living the same day over and over again. She would wake up. Go to work at the library, and then, at some point, she would meet Henry again. And Again. He would try and charm her. And then, when she went to bed, the next day, it was magically the same morning again. Hundreds and hundreds of times. "It was the Genie," Henry mouthed before he passed out. Lucy connected the IV meant to keep Henry alive.

And now to find that fucking Genie.

# Single

............................................................................................

Balbus felt the sheen on his external mucus sack as he slid from his tiny seat. His mind raced through the equations necessary to determine where he was right now.

Without even looking down at the dials and displays in front of him, he knew his relative speed, the gravity well shapes of all the celestial objects around him, and the direction of travel his tiny warp ship had been on.

Even among his exceptional people, The Rabondons, Balbus was considered very bright. He was a capable navigator but an even more proficient physicist, a scientist on many levels from a people who had evolved past a need for giant, bulbous complex bodies and, centuries ago, had manufactured these lithe and perfect unicellular forms that would last nearly forever and take up nearly no space on a planet so replete with people that its total population's mental power could reignite Rabondo's dying sun.

Balbus stood up a little taller and flowed smoothly into the adjacent release pod. He let the data jelly fill his mind with information on this new planet he had stumbled so clumsily upon and saw that it was many millions of years less advanced than Rabondo, but not really dangerous.

He opened his mind, one many times more powerful than Rabondo's centuries old supercomputers that had fought so hard to give them the stars. He primed himself for his favorite activity.

And learned.

The release pod opened and he felt himself washed out of the small opening on the bio ship, into a virile and fertile proto-soup of potential life that spanned this planet. His scanners fed yet more data to him as he moved through it, trying to take it all in.

In many ways, a new world was one of the most beautiful things a scientist like Balbus could ever find.

This world was filled with water and subtle gasses, swirling around to create a kind of possibility that Balbus found intoxicating and serene at the same time. Balbus thought about his home, the beautiful Rabondo, so perfectly tailored to him, so beautiful, yet still the center of a tense hyper storm of scientific activity, pressure, and goals, permeating every minute of his life.

As far away as he was, he felt the need to succeed, to produce, to build, falling away, leaving behind a blissful skein of wonder, an illusion of self sufficiency and wholeness that almost felt like a vacation.

He scanned the space in front of him for protomatter, tiny forms and there was so much filling up every drop.

That's when he saw her from across the puddle.

Balbus stared at her for almost a full minute as he considered the last few months in space. It was certainly lonely. She turned to him and he could almost see her cytoplasm behind a sleek and lithe cell membrane. What harm would one extra night here on earth be, anyway? No one would even know.

After all, he was single, too.

# Cupid

.................................................................................

Eden felt Daniel's lips for what felt like the first time. This was it. She realized that she loved him.  Her fingers wrapped tightly around his arm and her breathing became shallow.

The room began to spin and a tiny man in a diaper appeared just out of view, carrying an empty bow, restless, floating.

Despite herself, she let out a little scream.

"You see him, don't you?" Daniel looked around

"What the fuck..." Eden was completely unprepared for any of this.

"It's ok, I saw him weeks ago. It's ok. It's cupid.

"No way. That is not real."

"Oh, cupid is very real. I saw him when I first realized I loved you."

"I love you, too. But what's with the fucking naked baby?"

"Oh, he's not  a baby. I can tell you the whole story. The myth of cupid."

"I think I've heard that?" Eden was just a little confused, but she'd seen cupid on valentine's day cards and prom banners. He was the god of love? "Is it a good story?"

Daniel laughed. "It's a terrible story, but I don't care, i just want to spend time with you."

That worked. Eden slipped into the space made by the crook of his arm and listened.

"Ok, Venus is the goddess of love. And thousands of years ago, she had a fling herself, and had a baby with the Dionysius, the god of wine..."

"So, it was a good night..." Eden interjected.

"It absolutely was."

"Continue"

She named the baby Cupid and her grew up mentally very quickly. But physically, well, he was still a big baby."

"So, I've seen."

"Being the son of both the goddess of love and the god of wine, he grew up with serious boundary issues."

"That's not in the story."

"It is. You have to let me tell this. He grew up with some specious instincts. You know."

"If you say so," Eden laughed.

"So, he soon fell in love with this girl, a beautiful teenager from a neighboring town who was just visiting. He saw her and he couldn't help himself. He visited her room at night and turned her grape juice into wine. And when she was too drunk to consent, he had his way with her."

"That's pretty skeevy." Eden offered up.

Daniel agreed, "Yep. His parents both tried to teach him consent, but over and over, he proved that he didn't understand.

"This is absolutely not the story"

"It is. Until one day, they realized they had no choice but to punish him."

"Really?"

"You see, He's not the god of love, and he doesn't really have anything to do with causing it. He's just a tiny creature, really nothing more than a shell now, whose eternal curse is to forgo love himself, forever, yet to be there, in the flesh, to see the moment when every person on earth looks up, stares across space like we did…"

"and falls in love."

He kissed Eden all over again.

# Hunger

The thing that made this all so hard is that Rey and Michael never fought.

Not once.

Not since the very first day they met.

Rey was obviously new in town, trying to keep himself from staring, taking it all in like some kind of tourist. Michael had, again, obviously, lived here his whole life. He was jaded, if anything, hyperaware of every nook and crevice in the world around him.

But when their eyes met.

It was like electricity had passed back and forth between them. And it kept passing, sputtering, charging, buzzing, humming like the space between them was alive.

Imagine what it was like every time they touched.

Imagine the want, the need. Consider the feeling of having traveled so far and found, at the end of the journey, the very thing you were looking for. That is how Rey felt. And what made it so easy for Michael to slide in next to him, under the black eighteen hundred thread count egyptian cotton sheets and fall asleep with their mouths still open, connected, wanting.

They made love, but not the kind that we are used to seeing in our own bedrooms, respectfully passionate and so on. This was as though a vast and epic hunger was being sated, a kind of need that transcended the whole human race. Rey tore at Michael's clothes with a sort of savagery that even he couldn't explain, as though his famine-soaked eyes couldn't survive a minute longer without the sight of Michael's smooth brown skin, stretched taught over his six foot frame.

It was a beginning that neither one of them could have expected. And it made them drunk with excess, lost in each other, so often unable to even speak. But still Michael showed Rey his world. He took him to clubs and bars and rooftops where he tried to focus on the music, the food, the dancing, even the starry night, awash with speckled black rolling out overhead. But to each of them, there was no sight as resonant as the flesh of the other one, no desire more pervasive than the simple touch of their partner, the scent of them, the sound they made walking naked across the hardwood floor at night to step into the bed they shared since that very first night together.

And when the shooting star appeared over Manhattan, on that first night, they kissed in its raw light, even as Rey looked up and imagined it as a portent of endings and finales, the end of the beginning, he thought.

But not now, not tonight.

Rey had tried to put it out of his mind, when it would be - that first fight. In his heart, he knew it was approaching, on the trail of that incoming shooting star, when his people would arrive, in all their savage alien fury, to take this planet as their own and round up Michael's people to serve until each one was eventually cleaned, slaughtered, and eaten.

# Monogamy

..............................................................................................

No one believed that Ancho knew, from the start.

Right from the womb, some people say.

If you listen to him, he will tell you he knew at ten years old, definitely. He knew the situation and how it would play out. He knew everyone who would be involved. What he knew before that is possibly half-remembered, lost in the haze of youth. But after that, after childhood…

He knew it all.

But as he got older, it became clear that he wasn't going to make it without some help.

And that is how, at the young age of twenty three, Ancho became Aurelius, the most renowned and respected alchemist in the world.

Some will tell you that he invented the tools that would come to be used in the 12th century by all alchemists to prolong their lives. Every magical substance, every elixir, every potion that was used at the time to stave off death came from his hands as he worked tirelessly, putting that incredible mind of his to the test every morning, creating, innovating, inventing.

And as time went on, it became clear that this inexorable progression of old age had been held off at arms length for Aurelius, kept at bay by what seemed like sheer will. His only difference at birth may have been a knowledge that he kept locked in his heart, but his hands worked without fail in service of that knowledge, releasing it, increasing it, taking it into the next century.

And when the world saw the birth of real medicine, Dr. Aurelius was there, slowing the march of disease, building tools that would serve the body's defenses, tools that would soon spread across the world and save millions of lives.

Children came back to life from near death, families spent decades more with loved ones, and the doctor himself grew past the normal human age of infirmity and death, seemingly becoming stronger and healthier for each year passed.

He was widely beloved by both the newly emergent medical community and the people he helped, each new discovery shared with a waiting world where people died needlessly every day.

Dr. Aurelius clung to that as the centuries advanced. And, inside, the young boy known as Ancho, still a tireless romantic, reveled in returning lovers from death's door to the arms of the ones they loved for decades of life lived in joy. His journals kept notes and names and grew, year by year, in size and number that threatened to fill libraries with their wonder.

And every day he woke up strong, alive, He turned the page to the next day on his tiny paper calendar, hand drawn as a child.

And that's how Ancho turned the gift of knowing into a passion that lasted for centuries. To be born, knowing the exact time, date, and location your soulmate would be born was his curse, but the will to live long enough to meet her and love her...

That was all him.

# The Lamplighter of Precinct 7

......................................................................................

"Consider the pandas, for a moment. A global accident caused the death of the last few remaining Lamplighters for pandas and what was the result? What happened?"

Detective O'Donnel was really confused. He knew all those words, but could not make heads or tails out of that sentence that used them all together. "Is this some kind of preemptive insanity defense?"

"I am not crazy." Gira looked him over. She could see it. But he would never believe it. And that was good. "But you will persist in thinking I am."

Joe O'Donnel was a patient man. He had boxed in his youth - even going so far as to become the welterweight champion of his neighborhood - and it had taught him to put aside things like anger when it was necessary. He learned to pay attention. It taught him certain insights. And every bone in his body was telling him that this woman in front of him was harmless.

But she was also a potential felon.

Still, he listened.

"You might not get this, but since you are not a believer, I have a certain amount of freedom. I can tell you everything and you will never believe it." Gira kept him locked in her steely glare.

"That sounds good to me. I am not a man who believes easily. Why not tell me everything.?" Detective O'Donnel saw a crack in her persona, an in, and he wanted to exploit it.

"Have you ever heard of lamplighters?" Gira asked him quietly, looking around first for strange ears.

"You know, ma'am, I have not." O'Donnel's previous hopes fell a bit as he realized he was going to have to dig through a pool of nonsense to get at the location of the jewelry this woman had stolen."

"Across the world, Lamplighters are the ones who connect people who are destined, we put them together so that they can fall hopelessly in love." Gira looked up at his unbelieving face.

"Do you know you stole exactly five hundred dollars of jewelry? Enough to be a felony," O'Donnel asked, suddenly tired.

"Yes. I did. Because otherwise you wouldn't have gotten involved, Joe."

"My name is Detective O'Donnel. And are you telling me that you and I are meant to fall in love?"

Gira scoffed, "Of course not. I'm far too old. But here." She took the paper from him and started listing the jewelry stolen and where it was hidden back in her home.

Detective O'Donnel stepped into the hallway still holding the paper he had worked so hard to fill. He walked over to the dark-haired Korean woman standing next to the water-cooler to give her the good news about her jewelry, which could be in her hands again as early as tomorrow.

She looked up and smiled at him and he could tell she felt it, too, something altogether new to him, but wonderful at the same time.

He leaned against the cool wall and settled in for a long conversation.

# Gods of Grindr

...........................................................................................................

Neil was hot.

Like really hot. Everyone told him. And he believed it. He wasn't one of those people who thought that false modesty was a virtue. He worked hard to be his best, always.

These abs? Not an accident. Same with the glutes and every other muscle that rippled from under his baggy grey sweats when he moved around his opulent NoHo apartment as he worked his elaborately successful job from home.

Yup. Grey sweats.

He was smart. The extensive library full of books about nearly everything, alphabetized and placed delicately on spotless shelves he built himself perfectly to fit the curve of the outer wall of his place could tell you that. He was funny. A series of well-received nights last year at the laugh shack and the six or seven "funniest set" trophies sitting on that ledge over his grand piano in the den demonstrated that to anyone who cared.

Oh, and the piano worked and he was magnificent.

Neil stared at his own face in the bathroom mirror. It was perfectly symmetrical but with a very slight indent in his right cheek that worked just hard enough to render his face human and lovable and even slightly rugged. By any standard, Neil was a 10.

So why were so many "8"s swiping on him on Grindr?
Ok, maybe they weren't all eights but every time Neil had the chance to

open the app- designed to connect people for short term physical-type relationships, he saw nothing but a sea of eights, a few sevenss and then...

Everyone else.  He needed to up his standards. He went to the settings and began adjusting them.  And over the course of the next few weeks, he began to see some movement.

Today there was a Nine.

And now there were two.

Much better, for sure. But Neil himself was a ten. Was it too much to ask that he find another ten? After a while he started to consider something.

Years ago, he had heard the term Paragon. It meant, really, the best. It was a statistical reality. In a classroom, SOMEONE had to be the smartest, And if the class size got bigger, that didn't really change that statistical reality. Someone was the superlative.

What if HE was the most attractive person on Grindr?

On a whim, he adjusted his settings.

The next morning, there was one match.  He opened the app and saw the ideal profile. His body, flawless, his interests, talents, wants, experiences, all optimum.

And that face. Neil couldn't believe it. It just wasn't possible. But he saw what he saw. His new settings had created a match with a perfect 10.

He began the conversation, and set up a date.

He buzzed him in and met him in the mudroom, a perfectly chiseled, flawlessly dressed man wearing Neil's own face. He reached his hand out and said, in Neil's voice, "God, it's good to finally meet you."

But truthfully, he had him at "god"

# The Secret Origin of Suzie

Her name was Alimirtis, the legendary queen of death. You might remember her gold, black and green costume, clinging wet to her body while she lifted that giant freighter ship and sent it back to its home, with nothing but the power of her mind. She was magnificent. And to the heroes who underestimated her power, over and over, one at a time, she represented their defeat.

Even the ones who had never failed before.

Over the years, she fought so many heroes, putting down a whole generation of them, it seemed, in her battle for mutant equality and conservation of the earth. She battled Ultra to a standstill. She even faced the entire team of imagination-wave-empowered heroes known as Fourstar and prevailed.

She lost infrequently. And each time, she resigned herself to fight harder for her people. And for the earth itself.

She was only really a villain because they needed her to be.

But, by far, her most frequent foe would be the Undergrounder, the dark hero of Chicago's superhero group Nightwatch.

Undergrounder was born Enrico Santos, but his friends called him Enzo. As a baby, his family found they could not keep him, or even really find him half the time, as his mutant abilities, uncontrolled at first, made him nearly dissolve into any pool of shadow or darkness. He became invisible to the eye, intangible to the touch.

Impossible to hurt.

But Alimirtis did everything she could to try.

She captured him, immobilizing him with her mind, and bathed him in constant light. Still, he found a way to let the shadows consume him and deliver him victory.

She trapped him in a room built from illuminated and impenetrable materials. He managed to escape and thwart her plans again, this time in the most mysterious of ways, unknown to her.

He did what he needed to do, And he won.

Their battles became epic. And the papers wrote about them, magazines covered them, TV news shows made stilted and awkward recreations of their battles, attempting to share with the world the intensity of their clashes and how they nearly shook the world each and every time

They were the center of the battle between good and evil here on earth, for the longest time.
Until they weren't.

For her part, you could say that Suzie wasn't even there for her origin story, the night when two life-long adversaries realized that what they had been feeling for each wasn't hate, purpose, or even duty after all.

But love. Well, love peppered with a little bit of lust.

Suzie herself showed up ten months later, with a surprise of her own,.

Because who could have known that the first-born child of the most powerful mutant villain in the world and the beloved mutant hero of the night who fell in love in battle like that would have a child, adored by both of them, that would be so completely, absolutely, in every single way, so very unexceptionally human.

# The Unassailable Game of Love

They say there's no manual for love. Or really for anything.

But Jora wasn't sure that was true.

Simula9000 was sort of a kind of manual. In a way. It was a game that ran on the self-built computer sitting on Jora's desk, powered by the ultra fast processor she had installed herself and made visible through an exceptionally effective and overpowered graphics card that she recently bid for and won on Ebay.

You see, all Jora had to do was to use the character creator and make a perfect, classic, as real as possible version of herself, in the game, and then, because here is where the rubber hit the road, make a flawless version of Kyle, too.

And just feed them situations As time went on, with slight tweaks here and there, she was able to fine tune the game to become a near-absolute guide to how to make her relationship better.

It was really kind of genius, Jora frequently thought. Which made Jora a genius.

She looked down at her list of goals for this relationship and tried a few angles. If she wanted Kyle to propose, she was going to have to run a few scenarios.

And she did.

She started with some sexy ones. He loved it when she did that thing she does while he was driving. How about a night at a sex club, with her giving her all? She watched the tiny version of herself, all pink and nude, making tiny Kyle feel complete and wanted and loved. She made a tweak or two on the character's ass. It was maybe a little too round and classically beautiful. Jora had to admit she didn't really love her flat ass as much as she could.

This method had some hard truths to deliver.

It looked like a fun night, but it didn't go where she needed. She saved it for later. She leaned into romance. And after a few romantic situations, she watched Kyle get closer and closer to finally closing,

This was the way. She ran through almost twenty different scenarios, but none yet led to the ring. And then it hit her. She needed to plan a few romantic evenings in a row. One for him to get the idea. Then wait a bit, One for him to realize he wanted it and then, later, get the ring, And a perfect one where he had everything he needed to pop the question.

A week later, Jora looked at the ring on her hand, newly placed by Kyle after the single most romantic weekend of her life, and considered how she might take this to the next level.

She opened up the character creator for the first time in a long time and began to input all the characteristics she could remember from real life, building a near-perfect representation of Both Mia and Dean to place into the game house as she considered what their first night all together should look like.

# Gods

The origin of God is a sought-after piece of knowledge, but the truth is that gods are made all the time.

# Little Gods

........................................................................

Aunque prayed to the god of small spaces as he folded himself up and slid toward the reactor opening.

He felt the tickle on his skin of the caustic fire in the belly of the giant machine, the sign that he was being invaded, and he gave thanks to the twin deities that protected the traveler from illness, Norik and Golumbe. He contorted his hands in supplication, as well, to those minor radiation gods that might be watching, pleading with them to deliver his body from their grasp to the other side of the ship without illness, without death, hoping he had remembered each one in respect.

The tickle receded and Aunque's brain felt revitalized, refreshed, from the toxic rays all around him. He renewed his pace and searched for the broken cells, one by one. He reached out with his faith, as though it were a hand on a knob, and spoke, in his head, to Goryon Ko, the goddess of inspiration, to guide perfectly his hand and heart today and make his touch sure.

She provided him with the vision, so thought Aunque, to see, even in the dark recesses of the reactor base, the calls that required attention. The way these ships worked, if one cell burned out or was made inadequate by pressure or age, the cells around it would take on its burden and soon, if too many were inconvenienced, become itself burnt out.

The principle that was made to protect the ship from a quick and fiery destruction couldn't help but ferry it toward a slow and equally apocalyptic one if too many cells were damaged.

Aunque applied his spanner, the thick metal wrench in his hand, to the cell in front of him and, in a moment, it slowly faded back to its normative soft aqua blue glow. He began to move more quickly now as he identified cell after cell that required his attention.

Aunque set aside part of his mind to the task of thanking the goddess Thawkne for her service in making his eyes bright and his feet swift to the task before him. He slowly hummed a hymn to the minor gods that effected the air within the ship as well, to render it pure and fresh and able to feed him sufficiently to finish his task.

And as his faith carried him on, from cell to cell, his eyes filled with the cool aqua glow, rendering the long corridor beautiful in its light and function, welcoming and cool. Aunque smiled as he felt himself warmed by the grace of each of the gods of good fortune.

And as he turned the wrench one final time, the ship hummed to fervent life, seemingly healthy and ready for its journey. He breathed a sigh of relief, in his mind accepting the rush of praise from his supplicants across the ship who had exercised the wisdom to pray to Aunque, the god of impossible rescues, before he faded back to myth.

# The God of Elegant Purpose

....................................................................................

"I don't think you really understand how this works." Johari moved to the chair and made a point to ease into it as seductively as possible, sliding his lithe torso into the blue-black weave fabric of it and opening his sinewy legs ever so much to expose his god-like package.

If Cynthia noticed, she certainly didn't let on as she removed her black bra. "Oh, I understand it all. Trust me."

Johari laughed in a short spurt as thunder rolled outside the window seemingly in harmony with his every utterance. Yep, Cynthia thought. God.

"You want to fuck me in exchange for me making you a god?" Johari laughed again. Again, Houston weathermen, having testified to a rainless night, feared en masse for their jobs.

"Nope. Language is important." Cynthia pulled down her sheer black panties, exposing what most men would consider a perfect landing strip trailing down into an absolutely beautiful pelvic region from atop a belly that a Victoria's Secret model would envy. Cynthia was a beautiful woman, no doubt. Even Johari had to admit that. "I want to let you fuck me, any way you want, in exchange for god-like powers. I don't need to actually be a god."

"Well, the..." Johari sputtered, "The powers sort of come with the godhood part."

"Okay, whatever. I just want to do all that stuff you do."

"All that stuff." Johari sighed. He was the god of elegant and meaningful purpose. He was power incarnate. And he was catching himself staring at Cynthia's legs as they spread, revealing a cunt of pure beauty.

"Excuse me, I'm going to sort of get myself ready." She took two fingers and inserted them deftly between her nether lips, rubbing the top of her pretty pussy in slow, methodical motions.

"You don't think that's going to do anything, do you?" Johari slid into his most seductive voice.

"It always has. Remember, I summoned you"

She did summon him. Johari, aware and desirous of the power he always got from the adoration of men, could never deny a mortal the pleasure of his appearance. He survived and thrived through worship. And his power increased each time he was worshiped.

Cynthia laid back now and spread her legs. Johari could see she had no tan lines, suggesting to his imagination her, naked, spread out in the sun. He felt his godly body wanting and was reminded of how Zeus so often came to earth to carry off this or that maiden, filling her with his temporary affection before moving on.

He moved to the bed and put his hand under her belly, flipping her over to see her beautiful ass, reflecting the moonlight from outside the window. He penetrated her deeply with wild abandon.

And even as Johari's cock slid in and out of her lithe and wet pussy for the final few thrusts, he could feel the strength pour from him into Cynthia, his godhood exploding from his grasp, while his manhood exploded inside her.

# The Twin Gods of Filth and Decay

One of the things that history books try to hide is that being a god is not an impossible thing. In fact, humans become gods all the time.

Who hides these things, you say? I'm glad you asked. It's creatures like Dracos the Unmaker. Dracos has a number of jobs, one of which being to visit hapless humans who are on the brink of becoming gods and convince them otherwise.

If the universe is on the path to making them gods, Dracos, unmakes them.

Hence the name.

If you understood that easily, you can place yourself cognitively in a category substantially higher than Robin and Lindy, who, at the moment, are in the middle of their fifth explanation.

"Ok, so we aren't gods, yet" Lindy asked, honestly a bit confused.

"No. And you probably never will be." Dracos sat on the cleanest part of the couch he could find, his head tipped into his open hands.

"Aha. Then why are you here? Don't you unmake people who become gods." Robin seemed very proud of himself.

Dracos sighed and tried again. "Yes, but all that means is that I try to get you to see reason before that happens."

"Your version of reason?" Lindy offered up.

"Just THE version of reason." Dracos stood up, the unidentifiable blue-black stain on the couch following him. It was his stain now.

"You don't want to be gods."

"I don't know about that." Robin and Lindy had been friends since High school. They lived together because no one else would possibly want to live with them. They were both incredible slobs. And the last ten years of living together had only reinforced it. So much so that they had now become Homo Exemplar, humans who are beyond paragons, beyond the most of any other human.

The most at something.  And Robin and Lindy were the most disgustingly dirty.

Lindy picked at a bit of scrambled egg from weeks ago that had stuck to her leg while leaning against the chair, listening. She sort of liked the idea of being Gods.

Dracos felt a tiny bit of vomit rise in his throat as Robin peeled what looked like chocolate sauce from his butt...

And Stared

Dracos was confused. What he hadn't told them was that they each, in order to become gods, need to own at least one soul. Which, since they rarely ever left the house, would be impossible.

So how was it that the two slobs in front of him were now clearly glowing with unearthly illumination?

Robin lifted his left hand and sent a ray of deep blue light crashing into Dracos, sending him reeling in a wisp of smoke, dissolving, falling, collapsing into the  corner of the filth filled room just a few feet away from the broken down desk that held two soul sale contracts, one from Robin to Lindy and the other from Lindy to Robert, signed in blood, nearly impossible to read through the all over smudges of gunk.

# Hypnos Eternal

........................................................................................

"Do you know how disheartening it is to walk into a bookstore and find yourself as the very first entry in a book detailing lesser known Greek Gods?

Don't try unless it's happened to you. Just accept that you don't know.

Hypnos, the Greek God of sleep, stepped out of the Powell's bookstore and walked toward the Superdawg down the block. He made a mental note not to check his Wikipedia entry as today had already crashed his once respectable self Esteem and sent him questioning his whole life.

You live to be a couple thousand years old and you expect better for yourself.

He wished he could let it go. But being a god comes with a certain amount of self-aggrandizing ego. And Hypnos had it.

He made his way to the counter and ordered a Polish Sausage, Chicago Style, with a side of crinkle fries. Then, playfully, he told the man, "Is there a discount for Greek Gods?"

The man behind the counter was red faced and cheery, He shot back quickly, "I figure Zeus can afford to pay full price. " The cooks behind him laughed.

"Not Zeus," clearly he wasn't. Zeus still had that acne scarred face from his youth. It's like he was resisting growing up.

The man took the bait, "Well, you're not Venus or Mars, Nike, Hecate, Pluto, for sure." He eyed him up and down.

Hypnos managed a weak, "Nope"

"Eris, Asclepius, Dionysius, Aphrodite, Iris, Hecate..."      "

Hypnos was sort surprised the man knew so many of the more obscure ones, Hecate would be kind of impressed if she were here. He  tossed out, "You probably aren't that familiar with all the gods."

The man stepped up, "Sure, I am. I read that Edith Hamilton book in high school. I love that shit.

Hypnos sighed and took the Polish, paying full price. Really? Asclepius? he thought. God of Healing.

That was a deep cut.

He paid full price and took the Polish to go. The warm Chicago Afternoon was coming to a close as the sun dipped below the tree cover, spreading shadows out behind him that lengthened and darkened with every step.

He maneuvered the path into the well manicured Logan Square street and made his way causally, chewing with conviction, toward the shady end of the block where his tiny bed and breakfast-type hotel sat, lost in time, looking for all the world like a tiny Greek temple.

A knowing nod to the women at the front desk made him feel a little more special and he remembered that for later.

Hypnos leaned back on the top of the bedframe  in the sparse room and finished off the last of the polish sausage, It was really quite good and worth the excursion. He sighed and thought to himself, positively, that this may have really just been a bad day. As his head hit the pillow, he figured he would try one more time, in another thousand years, once he woke up again.

# Tyche in the Streets, Nemesis in the Sheets

The oddly colored man had won one election in the past and was still feeling that rush, the exhilaration. In a lot of ways, the world was his oyster.

It was a pretty raw and overripe oyster, filled with a number of deep-sea toxins and expired past all hopes of healthy edibility, but still. It was his.

This election, tomorrow, was going to mean everything. Would he be the leader of the free world, or would he be  ensconced in an orange jumpsuit and filed away with the rest of the business class criminal defendants too hapless to have hired a good lawyer or, and here's where the trunk of the tree sat, a good accountant in the first place.

Yes, jail loomed pretty large over that way. But the anything-goes kitchen of the white house sat here, in this direction, taunting him with its massive McRib knockoff sandwiches and plates full of tiny blueberry pancake pigs in a blanket.

His stomach rumbled as he stepped into the basement of his Florida compound. It used to be a resort for the hyperwealthy and even now, it seemed that every surface contained at least one beautiful dolphin etching.

"Ahh", thought the oddly colored man, many times a day, "Dolphins, my favorite fish"

"So, Ladies," he began, "What do you have for me?"

There, on the grubby floor, with only a steel bucket and pole to keep them company, sat his two prisoners. Tyche, the Goddess of chance and good fortune sat on her knees, opposite Nemesis, the goddess of brutal revenge. The man had won their services in a card game last month from a tiny little korean dictator too self-absorbed to notice his ham-fisted cheating.

"Well," began Tyche, with a weary sigh, "if you free me, I will create the good fortune you need to win this race. I promise you that you will never see the inside of a prison cell."

This was appealing to the man, who was concerned that he might have been too pretty for jail, and would certainly attract the wrong kind of attention. "I like where this is going. How about you, Nemo?"

"It's...nevermind." Nemesis had dealt with people like this in the past. She rose up from the floor to her full height. "I can ensure that no one will ever disrespect you again. I will bring down the sun and stars on the heads of your enemies, rain fire on their homes, have their children tortured and their dogs re-neutered."

That last one was sort of winging it.

The man stood there for just a minute. Tyche watched as his face grew dark, but split by a huge smile.

"Deal," as he freed the other God.

Nemesis rubbed her hands together, cold and numb from the restraints. She could absolutely help the oddly colored man with his revenge, but first, She thought staring wanly at his bald spot as he bent over to loose her ankles, a little revenge of her own.

# The Promise

Sh'uriko spread her toes in the silt that spread across the bottom of the slight pool collecting near the sleek mud-built church.

It felt good. It felt like the world underneath her feet was kissing her.

Bringing love.

She felt that this kiss from the earth below her was her religion. This was her excuse for leaving church early. She could worship A'laba from anywhere. She heard all the people crammed in the giant mud church singing, lifting their voices, and she felt their passion.

But she could feel it outside as well.

She could look up and see the glory that was A'laba traversing the sky. As she approached, becoming more beautiful than ever.

It was almost imperceptible, but today she shone, even in sunlight, as a dot just a few steps brighter than even Qu'sla'm the daily orb that gave them all light.

Sh'uriko took care to not look directly into their brilliance. She imagined them both, the twin gods that birthed everything good, talking, laughing, planning the future for all of the elder people - a future as bright and beautiful as they were. Just as all the people now planned their celebration for her arrival.

It had been months now since their priests had seen A'laba for the first time, a portent of something massive, for sure. The stories they weaved for the young ones brought all the peoples together in a powerful bond, one of hope and vision.

Sh'uriko had never seen the churches so full. And it was not just her immediate family and tribe, but every tribe, every kind of people from across the earth.

It was really beautiful, watching the churches fill more and more as A'laba approached, from a tiny dot in the sky, to a sphere that rivaled the holy sun. She wondered how large she was, how glorious. She imagined her in her own shape.

As all the people did. Wishing, thinking, worshiping, holding their children up in her light as she approached. Animosities between the different groups faded and even people that Sh'uriko had known since school who were angry, standoffish, distant in their own sense of tribalism, greeted her with joy when she came to church. There was a unity in the air that she had never seen before, one that connected everyone like different shaped pieces of the same puzzle.

But, behind that unity, behind the songs, each secretly hoped that their tribe would be the first to see A'laba when she came, the first to hear her speak. The old tribal habits were hard to fight and harder still to erase completely. But the people had lived long and endured despite it.

Sh'uriko spread her wings and took to the sky, her leathery iridescent feathers alive with the twin lights of her gods, still secretly hoping that when A'laba finally came to earth in just a few cycles, she would speak first to her family, the pteranodons and spread her love and grace to them first.

# Let Go The Storm

Millenia ago, God had unleashed a storm, a flood, that had nearly wiped human beings from the face of the earth. It took a long time for the people living at the time to believe it. And then, once it was done and the population of the planet dwindled it took even longer for man to forget.

But they did forget.

Asrit had grown up on this story and she believed it, even when the rest of the world seemed to fall into petty squabbles and dishonesties, infighting and corruption. She saw pictures, artist drawings, paintings of the horrors of that flood, how people by the thousands had paid for their iniquity with blood, falling, sinking, drowning, dying, alongside their families. And those images had drilled into her mind like a worm filling the center of an apple core, pushing out and spoiling the meat of the fruit as it went.

She grew up visualizing that event as though she were there, alive, watching, as throngs of people tried their best to reach safety but were pulled under and suffocated by the weight of God's judgment. And that visual, that idea had stayed with her for her entire life.

She tried hard to do the right thing every day and that showed, she hoped, on her face on that day when the voice of god descended and commanded her to build another ark.

The voice was powerful and confident and it told her tales about mankind's modern transgressions, each one sadder than the one before, stories about how humankind had turned their backs once more on God and had to be righted, to have their eyes opened again by the natural wrath of the all powerful, directing them to love justice, to work for goodness.

The voice gave her instructions and specifications for this new Ark, one that was smaller and more exclusive than the last, only to be filled by the people and animals most open and accommodating to God's new vision of the world. It gave her lists of people, manifests full of animals and goods, to fill the ark and to make it ready for its one and only journey, from the depths of chaos and sin to a new world where once again, the glory of God might be evident in every action of a grateful people.

And it gave to her a powerful purpose. Asrit was to be the new Noah, the new guardian and protector of the vanishingly small percentage of the populace that God himself considered worthy.

As the storm came and she set sail, the ship was warm and dry and filled with men willing to worship God as he wanted to be.

Asrit's heart was full while she opened the heavy wooden doors and let the waters fill the ship, smiling as the current swept her and everything she loved away, hoping against hope that once they were all gone that this evil god above would shrivel and die, as well.

# The Forest of Fire

....................................................................................

Keiko had learned, when he was just a baby, that every forest had a tree, revered by all the other trees, that would send signals to the entire forest and decide how it behaved, what it did, how it lived or died.

This tree, in the old stories, was called the God Tree.

And Keiko, left with no other recourse, was determined to find it.

Over the last few years, his city had burnt to the ground nearly every year, as massive fires that bubbled up from inside the neighboring forest washed across the tiny Japanese Village and left a swath of charred hopes, dreams and children in their wake. Kaiko was young, a firefighter adored by family and friends in his town, one who had already saved hundreds of lives through his bravery, quick thinking, and skill.

It made perfect sense that he would be the one to reach the God Tree and convince it to stand firm against the flames and fight them, giving the city a chance to heal and grow back to its former self. Every year, for the past five years, they had hoped that this would be the case that year, but each time, the other firefighters looked to Keiko in despair, sky darkened by soot and burning ash that was once the homes and lives of their friends.

Keiko set out, a backpack full of food and tools that might help him survive. And for every giant tree he encountered, bigger than the ones around it, he stopped to speak to it, only to be told that this was not the God Tree and that he should continue his search.

Many of the trees laughed at him, aware that his quest had little chance to succeed, some unaware of the position of the god tree except, in their minds, as a small, disconnected faraway voice.

Keikp opened his own mind and followed that voice, wandering deeper and deeper into the heart of the darkened forest, until finally, after months, he stood before the God Tree.

As reward, the tree talked to him, in his mind, and told him what he needed to know to start a conversation, in supplication, in the sight of its towering girth.

And so Keiko sat, in the growing shade of the God Tree, and talked to it about cities, and about people, about the world, and the skies and how desperately the people needed the light of the sun and how the gentle ecology of the forest was so im;poortant to the very survival of all of that.

He talked slowly, as the God Tree had taught him, every word a year, every sentence spanning decades, stretched out across the ineffable lifespan of the towering trees, as Keiko himself took root and felt himself connected to the ground through elaborate roots that split and spread and soon eliminated the need for words across a forest that never burned again, but grew greener and more elegant around him.

# The Sublime Glow

People like Marco who decide, without question, that it's their final day before they end it usually become happier, less burdened. They have a plan. They have an ending. And for people like this, just that is often enough to elevate their mood.

On the suicide hotline, they tell you to beware people who sound too content, too happy, because they are ready to go and they may just need an audience.

But the truth is that Marco wasn't happy. This was the lowest time of his life. He had lost his partner of fifteen years just last month to a particularly aggressive cancer. And Marco himself felt guilty that Jonah's passing actually made him feel artistically alive again, but his crushing money problems kept him from completing anything.

Marco was a shell, he felt, and it was time to let the rest go.

Pretty much everything that happens next is a kind of mythology. And that makes sense. Myth is the thing that takes over when living reason gives up. Myth is what people who decide to die abandon themselves to. This is why people who are in the throes of death so often see things that we are all positive don't exist. It's because they are sliding into myth, leaving this port that we consider rational and purposeful and entering a different space, one with different laws.

Now, Marco was a good man. In fact, one of the reasons he felt incapable of talking to anyone about how low he felt was that he, Marco was the one people came to. So many times he helped people find that last branch before they fell from the tree entirely. He was a quiet man, patient, and people took his gracious affection for humanity as a kind of nonjudgmental wisdom. They weren't wrong. It was just hard for Marco to tell someone his problems when he had always worked to lift people's burdens.

So he kept it inside. And planned to discuss this with the Marco he would find in the mirror that night. He made his way into the bathroom closest to his room and looked at himself in the mirror. And that's when he saw it.

It was hard to discern at first. But a pale indigo glow was visible, centered in the middle of his forehead. He turned off the lights, thinking it might be a trick of the light, but that only made it more visible. He could see it illuminating his face in the dark of the bathroom mirror.

Marco remembered a myth he had heard when younger. That the good you do in life made your soul glow, and when someone glowed sufficiently, God could not fail to notice them. This was Heaven, to be constantly in the sight of God.

Marco touched the mirror where the light shone through. He wondered if he could get the glow to be stronger if he went to work at the shelter tomorrow.

He smiled and planned.

# The Ice Church of Jingpo Lacus

Kids piled out of the hoverbus near the verdant shore of Jingpo Lacus, squealing and laughing. It was doubtful they would really learn anything today, but Iladro was willing to try.

He tried to talk to them about the Cielo Azul, the first shop to bring people here to live, near the lake. At the time, this green-blue and luscious lake was cold, frozen, shining like a mirror to the sky. And the atmosphere was four times thicker than earth.

It threatened to choke them.

And about how that tiny ship took almost three months to get to Titan from an earth that was falling apart and decaying, dying from misuse.

Iladro was a young man, back then, not much older than these kids he taught now, wrapped tightly in a space suit, missing his own home so much and landing in this place, looking back then like just some icy hell.

If there was water, at the time, it was trapped in giant blocks, like this crystalline ice church they found, facing the shore of the frozen lake. They stepped inside it so cautiously, wondering if they would ever see the home they left behind or even ever have a home again they could walk freely in, under an open sky.

He went on to tell them about their confusion, about how none of their records had ever suggested that people, at least not any kind they could ever recognize, had ever lived here. And from their confusion came the kind of reverence that made them make decisions possibly a little outside the scope of their standard operating procedure.

And that's when they decided to leave the structure alone and, before walking out, make an offering, a piece of the ship whose job it was to make them just a bit more comfortable. Something needed but they could reasonably survive without. The kind of thing humans had given to their gods for millenia, in exchange for just a tiny sliver of hope that they would intercede for them in a world that could be confusing and deadly.

A gift that those gods might appreciate.

"But, in truth, there were no gods of Titan. At least none that cared about the little ice church," Iladro explained.
'
"Wait," blurted out one of the older boys, "Then how did the explorers survive? And how come we can all live here now, if no one cared? Who helped us survive?"

"Oh, someone cared," Continues Iladro. This little Ice church was built as a test. We could have destroyed it easily, or ignored it. Or did what the explorers did. And leaving an offering, respectfully. Luckily, someone was watching."

"The Ti-marinians," The boy said unsurely. The people who were here first.

"Exactly. They wanted to know what kind of people we were. And I think we showed them."

"Did it really matter?" a girl in the back asked.

"Let's find out. Who here wants to meet them?"

A dense row of hands shot up.

# WORLDS

There is a secret beginning to every world
once you detemine which one you're on.

# The New Earth

···········································································································

"The problem with conspiracy theories is that they don't go big enough," Red said, shifting forward in his chair.

"Bullshit," blurted out Olive, the artist for "Sunscream," the hottest hero comic out right now. The audience laughed in unison. They wanted to like her. Red, not so much.

"That is a fantastic argument," spit out Red, not a little vindictively. His book, "Chronicles of Jupiter," sold probably half of what Sunscream did, but it was ORIGINAL, full of ideas and thoughts that came seemingly from the pure ether. He didn't want to put down her book, and he would certainly never do it publicly, but superheroes were kind of old news.

Olive continued, "The problem with conspiracy theories is that they embarrass all of us. I don't know about you, but all I want is to be taken seriously." Olive took a hit off of her vape and tried to look academic. Sunscreen was written, like most comics, at a twelfth grade level. Red didn't think she was a dummy, just that she had no imagination.

"You are free to believe what you believe," said Red, prepared to let it go.

"Waitaminute," spoke up Dean. He was the artist on the top-selling book "Atomic Children," who was constantly losing his comics code authority stamp for trying to sneak in nipples on all his characters. Red had counted seven nipples in the last issue. That was a lot of nipples for a book about barely of age superheroes. Dean was suspect. "What conspiracy theory do you think doesn't go far enough?"

Red paused. He really didn't want to do this, "We talk about the Mandela effect, about history being changed, altered. But we don't go big enough. I'll go further. I believe that we aren't the same race of people who populated this planet five hundred years ago."

The audience was split between uncomfortable titters and grumbling as Olive took the bait. "That is nonsensical. That's not something that could be hidden."

"Of course it is," Red continued, "We think of history as unchangeable, but it's not. There are new generations every 20 years to be taught. This gives the people in power massive opportunities to miseducate groups of young people. And there is evidence that even older historical documents are altered all the time. They recently discovered marks in hieroglyphs that suggested erasures."

The mumbling got louder.

Dean and Olive were unswayed. Both shook their heads. Dean looked animated, "This is why people come to these things and think we're all conspiracy nuts. But we're just writers and artists. Real people. "

Red sat back, satisfied, still feeling confident he'd made his case. The audience was skeptical but he remembered that at one point so was he. He snaked his third hand out from its resting spot on his chest and grabbed the cold drink in front of him, wishing, as he always did, that he had one irrefutable piece of evidence that would make all this go a bit easier.

# Under The Red Lights of Creation

In the beginning, the twin lights shone down on nothingness, illuminating the space where the people would one day be, filled now only with the massive raw mountains, bones and gristle of ancient giants and monsters before time.

Soon, in the unliving sand grew a woman, the first of the people, small and delicate and naked red, barely alive but surviving in the dying heat of that first dual light. She was tiny, at first, not much larger than the atoms that made up all things, the littlest machines of the universe, birthing every element in their crackling loom of creation, each space pregnant with new wonders for a new world.

As she grew, all the unliving places around her knew life from the first instance of her touch and she soon began to manifest the countenance of mother, progenitor, creator, infused with the forces swirling in her cells that made her at her own unlikely birth.

She named herself Hronpheer after the hush of the night's wind, breezes that brought comfort to her in the heat of the new world. She turned to that wind and tried to speak to it, but, like the sand beneath her feet, it had no understanding and could not connect with her.

So she did, for the first time, what all life eventually does and sought out other life to merge with and be as one, to experience the world from other eyes and know it better. She placed the parts of her that she knew were meant to bring forward life first against a stone, and, in the morning, found Krakora, a woman who was like herself, but where Hronpheer took after the wind, Krakora resembled the smooth and lithe, resilient stones from which she sprang.

It was not long before their differences, warmed and made vibrant by those things they shared, made them fall in love and bond, sharing their bodies and souls.

And from the union of their love was born a child, perfect in the eyes of her parents, brave and full of joy.

Krakora was grateful for the gift of agency and the power of her own life, as made real by Hronpheer. So she placed that lifegiving part of herself in the water and brought to her a third, Guluthuma, whose elegant blue skin and silk-like movements reminded them both of the life-preserving water around them.

They shared their love and, true to the way love creates, brought another child into the world, to bond and cling to the first. The three were proud and content.

And these two children grew big and strong, seething with power and able to see between the spaces of the universe, as they set out to fill their new world, spreading people across the expanse of their home.

They took nothing with them, except their names, the ones they had been given to honor, in the language of ancient forgotten giants, the twin lights that birthed all people, Fatman and Littleboy

# The Libraries of Elian

Admiral Crocket fingered the tiny orb in her hands thoughtfully as she descended down the lush aluminum stairs from the transporter room and headed into a spacious alcove topped by a giant symmetrical "Union of Planets" Logo. The tiny ball seemed to give under the pressure of her touch, ever so slightly.

The metallic globe had been sitting on her desk along with the invitation to attend this top-secret meeting earlier this week. Since then it had stayed with her, in her pocket, her hands, on the table beside her bed, as she struggled to figure out exactly what it was. It felt strange, alien, in her hands and she didn't know why.

The room was filled with chairs but empty except for an white envelope. She sat in the one dead center. As she did, a hologram of a woman sputtered to life in front of her. The woman was ancient and dressed in all the regalia of a high ranking official. She spoke.

"Admiral Crocket. Thank you for being here. I am ambassador Soluk. It's very nice to meet you."

"Nice to meet you as well," the Admiral began, unsure if this communication was two way and feeling not just a little silly.

"It's my job, as a member of this council who is preparing to die, to leave the knowledge in my care to someone who can take my place. There are documents detailing the specifics on the table but none of them include what I am about to tell you." The hologram continued.

She began to rifle through the folder in front of her, listening.

"A number of years ago, one of our ships found an abandoned vessel near the edge of our space orbiting a planet known as Elian. In it were thousands of the tiny orbs that you have in your hand. Upon investigation, it became clear that they were libraries, information depositories, that held nearly a universe's amount of data."

The hologram leaned in.

These libraries span all possible timelines. We learned that there have been subtle changes made to our reality. For the longest time, we have been concerned that our transporter technology actually kills people, who are then reconstructed on the receiving end with no memory of it. So we have kept meticulous records of transporter use. The computers discovered a connection between these records and the alterations.

"And that's when we learned the truth, from tapping the information stored in these tiny orbs. Unfortunately, it was a truth that nobody could really do anything about. Transporter technology is used all across the universe, by nearly every race and system. The chaos and disruption that would be caused by this information, if it became common knowledge, would be incalculable. That it wasn't the person being transported who died in a wracking painful death every time the device was employed, but everyone, in all creation, everywhere, only to be rebuilt again at the far side."

The hologram paused to take a drink.

# Seed

........................................................................................

The smallish silver alien packet fell through the ammonia night into thick, swirling eddies of liquid, sparking what would prove to be the very first proto-life form on the planet that had no name, only a number.

If there had been a camera at that exact moment, it would have laid to rest one of the most vibrant questions that the people of this tiny world had ever asked, one that every people in the history of the universe have asked.

Was there some outside hand at work in bringing life to this planet? And what was the intent of the creator?

Absent conclusions, we fill in the gaps in our own understandings with the kind of formative hope that answers the big questions for us. I mean, how many times have YOU considered it- the idea that we may share common ancestry with the other species of the universe that rise up around us. And even this question, posed like that,. Seems to carry a mandate of cooperation, of trust.

A promise of brotherhood.

There are similarities in the humanoid races. That much feels reasonable and clear, doesn't it? The subtle arc of their bipedal backs as they dip to create the waist, then torso, ridged with muscles meant to carry us upright into the day. The open, hairless forehead, sometimes adorned with some emblematic organization of ridges or crests, meant subconsciously by facial recognition parts of the brains across the universe to brand each separate species of people and alert them to the presence of outsiders, ones that might threaten the tribe.

And the elegant carpal split of fingers as they grew from the bottoms of animate arms, placed laterally, symmetrically, on each humanoid, differing possibly in number and in construction slightly but always fanning out into hands, used to build, to love, to carry children, these were universal as well.

We can see, you might think, some convergence, some universality, even in the shapes of brains, the forms of them, and their output. Languages fall back on familiar themes, models for their construction, methods of creating meaning, each one of which reduces to some visual medium to carry long distances and into the auditory world for immediate translation by the creatures around us.

That is incredibly telling, in itself, even if we discount the linguistic similarities extant, ones that enable advanced cultures to easily build translator devices for interested people.

There would be days that provided answers for these people, even if they were mostly predicated on circumstantial evidence and speculation.

But four million years from now, this would be the pregnant moment of generation that teachers and scientists, kings and leaders would celebrate as the very first stirrings of life on that stoic planet, one that would by then be teeming with possibility and divergence, seeded by the hands of a prolific creation force with that tiny metallic package of potentiality, loosed from beneath the toilet section of that distant traveler's ship, and passed into eternity.

# This Time

........................................................................................

This time she had positioned herself to be his lover. And, from what she understood of Matt's mindset, she would likely soon be his wife, which was a situation that would enable her to stay on top of the situation, for sure. At least until he understood who he was.

The entire thing was unbelievable. Tia would have never believed it herself, except that lately she had begun to remember. It was coming back to her, all of it.

The first time she could remember, Matt was her coworker at a real estate startup. She answered phones while he sold shabby walkups until one day, while she sat in the car next to him, after accepting a quick ride home, his side of the car was flattened by an oncoming six wheeler. And suddenly, she was back to the beginning.

She found herself six years old, on the day that, hundreds of miles away, Matt was being born. She lived her life again waiting to encounter Matt. And she did. This time as an insurance salesman in a local firm where she had been working for over a year. It seemed they were destined to meet.

In every revision, Matt would eventually learn who he was.

He was a maker, one of the rare creatures in the universe who serve as a lynchpin of reality. He was born to live and shepherd reality, so, if by some accident he died. It would just, well...

It would all start over.

In previous iterations, Tia was his friend, his roommate, even his business partner. She was able to create fortunes with the knowledge of the timelines his death created, but invariably they would be wiped out once Matt died again. The longer she could keep him safe, the more she could enjoy what she was able to build.

And she enjoyed the comfort that wealth could bring.

But time after time, he would die, leaving her to start over again, as a child, now with a complete set of memories, triggered by her closeness to Matt at his death. It seemed the closer she got to him the more she would remember. And the more it would hurt when he died once more.

Matt was a good man, although quick to anger. He was a man of principal and it was probably inevitable he would confront that stranger hitting his child across the face in front of the restaurant that night, opening himself up to the knife the man carried in his left jacket pocket.

Tia watched while Matt dropped to the ground.

As he died she waited to fade away, to revert once again to six years old, to live all this over again, but that didn't happen. She reached out sadly and realized how much she had grown to love him. And in the coming weeks, she would miss him desperately, more and more each day, it seemed, as her belly grew rounder preparing for the birth of his child.

# The Book of War

I'm told that it's my job to document what is happenning and tell the story for the future.

Which is crazy because as of last week, my job was to sweep up and clean the soft serve machines at the dairy queen on Roosevelt.

So that, right there is something to document.

Today, we are going to war and I don't know with whom. Today we're going to breathe life into the new world and I don't know what happened to the old one.

Today, I am Metatron, of the Angelic Legion and yesterday, I swear, I was an atheist slightly failing history class and trying to convince my parents to let me stay out until midnight.

I'll tell you what I know because I have to;  it's my job now. But there's so much more I don't know.

The storm hit this morning, about two hours after all of us had gotten to school. It came out of nowhere and it was ferocious, unstoppable. Lightning had set the school gym on fire while the one hundred knot winds ripped the top story classrooms open and the roof to shreds. I watched just about everyone in my class killed in some horrific way and then, finally, died myself, when the thick upper branches of the tree that was planted by the Alumni society twenty years ago stabbed its way through my chest like a chopstick traveling attached to the front of a motorcycle.

A big one.

Right now, as I write this, the earth is being destroyed by a war that we humans had nothing to do with. There are voices in my head telling me all this and affirming, over and over again, that I have to be the one to tell the world.

Or what's left of it.

When God made the Angels, he installed a failsafe, a method in their construction. You can say, in programmer's terms, that it was a back door. It was meant to prevent what happened with Lucifer from ever happening again.

And Lucifer never stopped trying to figure out how to "hack into" that subroutine- to destroy all the angels in one pass.

Until this morning, at 9:45 CDT when he did it. And every angel made since the dawn of time was suddenly unmade.

The result was chaos all across earth, as every disaster, misfortune, and poor luck that was staved off by the gracious will of the angelic body was suddenly visited upon mankind. And without the angels he had relied on for so long, God himself disappeared.

This was only just a few hours ago. I'm watching the people I go to school with learn how to use their new angelic abilities, how to fight, how to lead, to make sense of it.

All I know is that the force at work that is forging me and my classmates into the new angels is not the God we're familiar with. It's something else. Something Bigger.

And it's coming.

# There Are No Monsters on Reglus 4

"There are no monsters on Reglus 4," Auren had famously messaged back to Earth almost nine years ago to the day.

This was met with widespread celebration across the entirety of Earth, from a weary populace ready for solutions, not problems. The planet had been poorly shepherded and now those same stewards, big businesses and massive corporate sponsors, were helping to spread humanity to the stars, hoping to prevent the extinction of their entire people.

Reglus 4 was one of six planets that had been targeted for colonization by the corporate committees, who had chosen each for its speed to market, not for any natural ease by the founding colonists, sent off in clunky and awkward ships, made unwieldy by constant adherence to the bottom line, and made dangerous by a system that had never given much thought to the peaceful survival of the occupants.

So if Auren had felt old on the surface of that strange blue-green world, after ten years of travel, five years of full-on battle with the local fauna, and nine full years of leading this group of colonists, that could be expected.

But he didn't.

Auren felt alive today as he stripped the flesh from the body in front of him, powerful, even invigorated by the daily hot and cold cycle of this severely alien planet - one they had claimed as their own through blood conquest.

Ok, that may be a bit dramatic. When Auren and the rest of the two hundred and twenty seven colonists had arrived, Reglus 4 was a human habitable planet well within the close-in goldilocks orbit of an M-Type star. It would be quick to convert this planet to an amiable living situation for the colonists.

But first, they would need to dispose of the native monsters that populated it.

They were bipedal and smaller than humans. But they were quick and had long, elaborate knife-like claws and sharp, ragged teeth that contained a venom that could kill from just a slight scratch. They prowled the planet both night and day and required a consolidated effort on the part of the colonists to kill. Their faces, though, looked altogether too human for comfort. This required that the colonists put aside the petty sentimentalism they carried with them from Earth. Reglus 4 required a more cosmopolitan approach to living. If they indeed wanted to live here.

And they did. These corporate-built ships were not designed for a return trip. If they weren't able to tame this planet, they would have no choice but to die, themselves.

Auren packed the meat tightly in the coolers he would need to store it. He felt a twinge of sentiment for Alex, flayed out on the table in front of him and his two children, but that soon went away. He was fairly sure he could fend them off. Besides, they would understand. They were born here on this planet where man had become so proficient at killing that it was just second nature.

# This World of Water

There was a promise made by the Talokians when they delivered the imaginarium. This device, a small white hall that showed people their wildest dreams - anything they could imagine, was, when fully activated, capable of manifesting those dreams in reality.

The hope was that, through our friendship with the Talokians, through time, through understanding what our dreams and hopes really were, we would become ready for the full power of the device.

That day was superseded by the explosion of the machine, one day in August, after its constant use caused it to be run nonstop for nearly a year. The resulting fallout, called the imagination wave, delivered their heart's desires to people all over, directly in the path of the event.

And now, some five years afterward, we are still managing the aftermath of this event. Superheroes, Lottery winners, sexual heroes, superstars, lavish homes, brilliant inventions, all of these are easily charted and followed by the Bureau of Imaginary Activations (the BIA).

But there is still a lot we don't understand.

And one of those things is the Current.

A few years ago, engineers discovered that there was a vast, almost endless world about a mile below the streets in major cities all over the world, completely covered in water. This discovery was made simultaneously in multiple cities where it was found that these connected worlds contained every manner of flora and fauna conceivable for an underwater ecosystem.

It had all the earmarks of an activation by the Imagination wave but we were unable to track down who had imagined it. Who would have dreamed into existence an entire world of water below every city?

I want to insert a personal point here, if i can. I recognize that my own agency refuses to acknowledge my conclusions here and that is the reason for this letter. Enclosed is the proof of everything I am asserting and, if considered without prejudice, it may be the greatest revelation in the history of our culture.

I don't expect to be believed, but there is an enormous amount of solid proof here, backed up by marine biologists and scientists all over the world.

We can use the locations of events to sort of zero in on the people who imagined them into life, very often. The wave had perceivable vectors and a smallish radius in which it was active. Many times we have also been successful tracking people's dreams, wishes, hopes, through their social media presence, although I confess, in this case, that led us nowhere.

I managed to track down the vectors and triangulate the match that lit the fire of imagination responsible, following it to a building directly in the path of the wave, a restaurant with only seven tables called Itto Sushi, in which a tank containing a number of Octopus sat, cephalopods that I believe, changed our entire reality based on a dream they had together.

For more background, please contact me personally,

Noah Richardson
Austin TX
Ex BIA

# Warriors of Monticello

Adina watched the timescope in horror as she made adjustment after adjustment. No matter what she did, however, the results were the same.

In Adina's reality, the earth was a living force. And, over the centuries it had raised up champions, called Numina, from the dead to fight for her children. But in timeline after timeline, Adina watched as the Earth's spirit died young, early in its development. And these dead worlds never raise up champions.

Sickness and decay, war, Holocaust, slavery, this was the result of the lack of intercession from these dead alternate earths. Humans died out entirely in some, destroyed by the aftermath of the Toba Volcano explosion. On many worlds Fascist dictators spurred on by a group known as Nazis infected the timelines, ruling for decades in some and centuries in others, causing billions of deaths and worlds full of suffering.

And one of the most horrifying was world slavery, spurred on, in no small part, by American Colonial chattel slavery. Without the efforts of a young Yoruba champion on her own timeline, Adina saw entire continents turned ugly and debased by slavery. Hundreds of years of injustice and pain inflicted upon people of color and thousands of years of cultural cruelty created by mainstream culture, carried onward by dominant whites so much so that often, in timeline after timeline, it led to the sinking death of the entire planet.

The widespread implications of this colonial chattel slavery were so severe that only a rare planet in a rare timeline survived.

Adina turned to her computer to track potential inflection points, discovering one that stood out, again, in nearly every timeline.

One of the architects of American society was Thomas Jefferson. He was a statesman, a thinker, a writer, responsible for many of the documents that defined the American experience. And on his plantation, Monticello, throughout the course of his life, he claimed to own over six hundred human beings.

Adina shuddered to think about it.

By sending back to these timelines weapons, tools, technology, that could be used by the oppressed in Monticello, she saw that the effects could be undone. These six hundred people, with access to the right materials, could change the world, over and over again, in every timeline. They could make a difference that would lead to real lasting peace. And the cost, at her end, would be minimal.

Adina sent her findings upstairs to the materials and resources committees. She received an affirmative response even faster than she thought. The timeline collective was anxious to create real good here.

Adina ran the calculations to ensure that her changes would remain. People frequently talked about temporal battles where people on both sides of an issue made their own subtle timeline changes only to find them reversed by the opposition. She smiled as she saw that this would not be a problem.

Because, as it turned out, no timeline hobbled by the horrors of slavery had ever risen to invent time travel.

# The Proposal

It may have been the butts that sold it in.

The butt is really a magical sort of concept. This idea of a rounded backside that is so magically multipurpose, you can use it to evacuate, you can use it for pleasure, you can rest on it. It can be as alluring as a Jamaican artist twerking in a dancehall music video or as comforting as a place to lay your head after a long day, watching movies with your girlfriend,

It can even be naughty.

"You never know what is going to sell through a proposal," thought Yawen as he tried to organize his desk. To be clear, this was a desk that would never know real organization. Yaween was a real architect, in every sense of the word. He saw the big picture.

It was easy to lose sight of the little things, really.

But, in the bigness of it all, Yawen was a superstar.

He knew how to devise ecosystems that were incredibly powerful, sustainable, that would last in a timeless and constantly renewable way. He knew construction, he knew biology, he knew organization, He understood Feng Shui long before it was a thing, and identified top selling colors long before anyone had even come up with names for them.

Like phthalo green, a deep, dense but vibrant color, more intense than Viridian Green (pg18) and more saturated than a forest green, but redolent in the somber shades found in the deep canvas cover of a light-strewn forest floor.

Or Umber, a darker and more complex ocher, yellows and browns merging together to form a coppery dense testament to the beauty of native neutral colors splayed haphazardly across the beauty of creation.

He knew physics, in his way, math, to a degree, and, if you ask him directly, was really a hell of a writer.

But more than anything, this guy could rock out a proposal.

We live in a time that might go down in history unironically, as the Powerpoint Era, a time that is marked by the need to create presentations- proposals- that outline everything you mean to do verbosely so that someone, with some degree of authority, will allow you to do these things.

And we think of this dynamic as a unique facet of modern human life, forgetting that it's been this way since the dawn of time, since long before the advent of powerpoint, the birth of Microsoft, or even the first computer. We forget that people with vision have been forced to lay out their plans to visionless superiors in hopes that their hands will be freed to execute in every culture, every people, since humankind began.

And, from the looks of it, long before that, even, Yawen thought.

So, in the end, while Yawen's beautiful proposal was a huge part of why the Earth project was greenlit by the universal Construction and planetary maintenance group, a lot of people still think that it was the butts that really sold it.

# HORRORS

Daily, this world brings for horrors of every kind
and today is no exception

# That Shape, Though

Bill had no neck.

Or, conversely, he had too much neck, the fact of the latter often creating the illusion of the former in the eyes of less discerning people.

This, combined with the general roundness of his head, tapering to a near absence of chin blurred what should have been a healthy distinction between head and neck, deemphasizing where one began and the other ended.

Additionally the 2 lateral whisps of shoulder that flanked his upper torso gave credence to the theory, imagined by Bill's parents in quiet nights at home, that some callous, uncaring creator god had, rather than becoming directly involved in the creation of shoulders for Bill, merely whispered "shoulders" to the half made fetus and sent him on his way.

The overall effect was jarring, most especially when coupled with his overlarge feet that, due to a boating accident at a young age, tended to jut out at right angles to either side, supporting a silhouette that created an uncomfortable shadow on any far wall.

It wasn't so much that you could easily, seamlessly, without lifting your hand from the page, draw the image of a buttplug, flared base and all, over a picture of Bill, it's that it was only with some difficulty that you could refrain from doing so.

And those same parents, perhaps in a moment of sympathy for those who would one day have to name this forbidden shape and characterize their own child, chose to name him "Bill," creating a rare opportunity for near-perfect alliteration.

Or at least that's what people thought when they invented the name, on more than one occasion, of "Buttplug Bill."

Andrew chuckled a little under his breath, considering that shape as it spilled over onto the far wall now, imagining a marker in his hand as he drew a classically shaped buttplug with one hand. But even that small bit of whimsy had a price. He coughed up blood, sending it spraying out onto the already blood-filled floor to virtually no effect. More of his blood was now staining the Spanish tile of his ranch villa than had chosen to stay In his body.

And that was, he thought, medically, unadvisable. He knew now it was too late.

"It's not yet too late," piously intoned Bill, almost as if in direct opposition to the unspoken thought in Andrew's head. "You can still tell me where the money is." Bill pulled the magazine from his Glock and slowly filled the chamber with six bullets, replacing the six he had recently placed into Andrew's taught, toned, body to get his attention.

"I don't have it," spat out Andrew, fearlessly. He knew, as did most members of the underworld, that few men took a visit from Buttplug Bill and survived to tell of it. He had resigned himself to death hours ago. But, looking down, he could see that Bill's oversized feet were dragging thick blood trails across every surface.

And that thought got right up Andrew's ass.

# Cell 44

It started as a dream Knox had had during the early days of the invasion.

He dreamt about a man, just like any other human being, tearing into the Beetles with only the power of thought, ripping through their defenses, destroying them easily. Armed with only a 2 foot padded backpack, he waded into battle and the enemy dispersed.

And they died.

Knox had clung to this dream as the invasion now dragged on into its twelfth year. His people were losing. Humans were no match for the Beetles with their seven foot tall multi limbed steely carapace covered bodies and advanced technology. They would soon lose this planet.

Unless he could make his dream real.

Knox stepped into cell 44. Of all the cells, all the experiments, this one was most promising. Knox conjured up his dream again, trying hard to remember every sight, every sound, every piece that could draw him closer to the finish line. If he didn't have an answer soon, everything he knew would die.

Knox didn't enjoy his work. But he knew what was at stake.

In front of him was a shell of a man, a volunteer named Kendrick Jameson, twenty four years old. He was a marine,. A hero in his own right. And Knox had been torturing him for months. Crimson wrapped stumps squirmed now right below his torso where his legs had been. Knox had cut those away, inch by inch until there was barely enough left to move. The skin of the marine's face and chest had been pulled off, revealing purple muscle beneath, while each arm was eviscerated, stripped like you might peel a carrot, devoid of muscle or sinew at all, really just animate bones that slapped against the metal gurney with dark clacking noises as he writhed beneath the pain.

Knox knew, in his heart, that the secret to unlocking the mental abilities that all humans had imprisoned inside them was need. That torture and fear of absolute death and dismemberment could open the pathways to those abilities, and release the kind of power needed to win this war.

Jameson had endured so much. But Knox could almost feel a kind of pressure mounting, a power building, much like a storm cloud waiting to deliver God's own wrath on a Tennessee trailer park. The air in the room was charged and Knox felt closer than he had ever been to a solution.

He lifted the knife and carved the last of the flesh from around Jameson's chestplate, hearing him screaming in his head. Just as the scream reached a crescendo, he saw it.

The metal plate holding him down came spinning across the room and lodged itself into the wall. Jameson had done it. The pain and inhuman abuse had finally triggered the needed areas of his brain to activate with a pulsing power that could win this war.

Now, if Knox could just carve away a bit more flesh, he would fit into the backpack.

# Blank

Shana had chosen a bustier body than hers today. This blank was a 36C with perfect half-dollar sized brown areolas and groomed down there with a dark, tightly wound landing strip that dipped into a fully shaved bottom rounding between her legs to what she imagined was a classic Brazilian ass.

She ran her fingers over the tiny almost blonde soft hairs on the body's belly and tried to remember what they were called.

"It's called vellus hair," offered up the operator, as he powered down the transference machine. Everyone asks.

Shana dismissed that to some part of her brain for later retrieval. "This body does anal?" she asked boldly

"This body contorts in every way, and if you relax, it will comfortably accommodate large object insertions, anal sex, pain, and it has no gag reflex." The operator was a handsome black man with a thin, well cared for beard and Shana started to feel the body's natural response standing in front of him naked. Unlike her own body, this one was incredibly responsive. The tops of her thighs were wet as the operator demonstrated his last assertion by putting nearly his entire hand down her body's throat.

Thirty minutes later, Shana wore that body out in the warm summer afternoon, in a sundress that let her enjoy the warmth of the operator's cum dripping from her ass that had, indeed, managed the act without a hitch. She stared at her new face in the window of a dress shop and planned the next two days with a body that she could really enjoy without consequence.

Shana was wealthy enough, but this was still a luxury to her. It cost her nearly three months salary every day to be the exceptional woman in this body that drew stares from everyone. There were so many things she wanted to do and her plain and inexperienced flesh would never accommodate them. First of all, she thought, would be the orgy tonight, something she had always dreamed of but never done.

Her own body, languishing in a liquid bath, unoccupied, back in the transference center, was something people rarely noticed, pale, doughy, and frequently sickly. This raw sexual energy she felt now was new and it reminded her that this was a good idea, something she needed.

That night, she felt that even more strongly. There was a power in this body. She was fearless. She felt open to every fantasy. . She sat boldly on a waiting man's cock while another entered her from behind.

As she let herself go and enjoyed the immersive feeling of being double penetrated, she recognized, for the first time, that there was something else in there with her, a kind of growing presence. She closed her eyes and let it rise to the surface, giving in, fading into the recesses of the brain so far, she hardly realized it when her nails dug into the man's neck, sending his warm blood in waves over her naked breasts.

# Alone

.......................................................................................

Jacob woke up Saturday morning to a quiet house and an email from an unknown address ending in ".gov"

Enclosed was a video. Putting his phone back in his pocket, he descended the stairs. He knew enough not to click on unsolicited videos.

No one was in the kitchen, no one to battle for his place in the bathroom, no one watching cartoons in the living room, He glanced again at his phone and saw that it was later than he expected.

Jacob wondered how he had missed everyone this morning, when a distinct "ping" alerted him to another email. This one from the same address, also with a video.

He walked out the door, concerned for a moment that he was on some new spam email list that would take him some effort later to unsubscribe from.

The streets were empty

He looked down at his phone. Again, a gentle tone alerted him to a new message.

He opened it and began to watch the video.

In it, a woman sat at a desk with a serious expression on her face. She began, "Jacob Sperling, please, if you can, watch this entire video."

If this was spam, it was the most custom, direct market spam he had ever gotten. Jacob Sperling sat on the steps and listened.

"There is a Christian myth that is not terribly well supported by the Bible and yet it has managed to weather the centuries and become ensconced in the minds of people who think religiously. It is called the rapture."

This Jacob knew. It was something his mother talked about. He himself was not religious. He started to get anxious.

"I belong to a government agency that is tasked to keep track of this particular event, in the understanding that it HAS happened on a few occasions throughout history. In a way."

Jacob looked up. If this was spam, or a prank, it had just become legendary. Did his entire family hide and then spoof him with this email? His brother Todd would have the technical knowledge to do that.

But Todd was not funny.

"Three times, in fact," the woman continued, "And each time, humanity was able to manage it, control it, and, eventually stop it." The woman on the video became very serious. "Jacob, we are asking you, do not leave your block."

He looked up. The sky had darkened. He saw the planes moving mysteriously overhead and squinted to get a better view. There was no way for him to tell they were drones, operated from hundreds of miles away by volunteers who knew the day would come, possibly, that they would have to drop a bomb on a teenage boy.

God, as well, has been known to move in mysterious ways, And one of those ways is to create, every few thousand years, someone with the natural ability to send everyone around him to heaven, an ability that can't be contained, and, unfortunately for Jacob, can't be controlled.

# Where Monsters Breed

........................................................................................

This is one of those discoveries that makes a kind of sense if you let it. I'm not ashamed to admit it hit me like a bit of an a-ha moment.

It started at work, where I'm a Janitor. I got that job at the magnetic resonance institute out of high school and they gave me a ten percent pay increase every year. So here I am now, thirty-six years old, one job my entire life, mopping the floor all night for almost ninety thousand dollars a year.

So, honestly, I ever thought about going anywhere. Until this week.

I should back up a little. I had no idea what this place did, until I started here, so i have no expectations that you understand. It basically uses magnets and magnet related technology to track the brain waves people have during sleep, helping them sleep better. That's sort of the abridged version.

People come in and pay and get tested, put on a magnetic hat and sleep better. Don't laugh, it works.I mean, they've been here, in this building, for twenty plus years.

And that's where most of their income comes from. Just people wanting a good night's sleep.

The rest comes from patents on the discoveries they make while helping people sleep. When I first heard that, I couldn't really imagine what those would be. I mean, what kind of inventions are they creating? Nothing I see at night when I mop up.

First of all, they study those brain waves I mentioned. There are two groups of delta waves occurring during REM sleep- the kind you have when you dream: slower waves at <2 Hz, recorded in medial-occipital regions, present in both NREM and REM sleep, and faster REM-sleep-exclusive, fronto-central/occipito-temporal "sawtooth" waves at about 2.5–3 Hz.

Yes, I admit I copied that out of the MR manual.

It's mostly waves generated by the amygdala. But, there is activity in the anterior insular cortex, another region involved in cardiovascular regulation. I overheard that one.

These two areas of the brain, when working together, can be really powerful. Apparently, this is where a lot of the research dollars have gone. What does triggering these two areas do?

I'm glad you asked because it's a big part of why I'm out of here.

Let me give you a what if.

What if human dream sleep is meant to be a protective thing. Our ancestors slept outside, right, where animals and aggressors could get them. So what if when the body was stimulated during REM sleep, the Amygdala and anterior insular cortex would fire, creating a means of escape.

This would allow a sleeping human to get away from an attacking bear, or another tribe attacking, for example, easily. Now try and follow me.

What if it created a portal that opened up right below the person, hiding them in a different dimension? And now, because we sleep in beds, that portal opens up below.

Right under the bed.

# The Extraterrestrial

Emmy was nearly fifty years old when the ships landed and tiny green men joyfully poured out onto the white house lawn. They had signaled their arrival and began by giving gifts to human leaders that were every bit as awe-inspiring as you might imagine, coming from a civilization so far advanced from our own.

The first was a replicator-like device, a three-dimensional food printer. It used ambient particles in the air and water to create food. And not just simple dishes, but elaborate ones, like cheeseburgers, lasagnas, etc.

This, on its own, elevated and reinvigorated the restaurant industry while simultaneously helping to alleviate hunger in developing countries all over the world.

These people, known as the Talokians, were friendly and compassionate and wise. They had sent an envoy years before, one that Emmy had actually met and befriended. And they trumpeted, to the people of earth, that they were pleased with the messages that envoy sent home, about guileless children who played with him and parents who dressed him and made sure he ate. These messages took decades to reach Talok, but the stories had become legendary.

And, at today's ceremony, Emmy and her friends sat in positions of importance, respectfully elevated by the Talokians as friends of Talok.

Of all the devices they gave humanity, though, none was as resonant and fascinating to the population of earth as the Imaginarium. It was a three thousand square foot white room, rounded at the corners, that was always clean, never blemished.

But that wasn't what made it special. Entering the room showed you, in detail, what it would look like to get your heart's own wish. Your deepest desire, your fantasies, your aspirations and goals, all played across the room while you were inside.

The Talokians joked that when humans were ready they would remove the "training wheels" and the imaginarium would deliver on all those promises. Emmy wasn't sure she believed that.

She tried to do the math in her head of how long it took for the messages to get to Talok. Her blood turned cold realizing that they had not yet received the last few messages sent all those years ago when Egg, that young Talokian, had visited earth and played with her and her friends.

She heard the recordings that the people from Talok had brought talking about the fun they had had. Crowds of people listened in and heard her voice, as a little girl, playing dress up with the young Talokian, riding bikes, and just being children.

Emmy's first visit to the Imaginarium showed nothing. Because what she hoped for, more than anything, was nothing. A part of her wanted nothing more than to die.

You see, Emmy had been waiting decades for this moment. It had begun differently than she thought, but she felt sure she knew how it would end. When the last of the messages from earth finally caught up and the Talokians discovered how humans had killed their little Egg.

# The Left

It started with some little drawings I would post on facebook. People liked them. I would sometimes get thirty or forty reactions and maybe a few comments. Which, for me, was great.

It felt good.

But I didn't draw them. I'd wake up in the morning and there would be one there, at my desk. The funny thing was they looked so much like something I WOULD draw. I felt an affinity

A connection.

I used to draw a lot, before the nuns at St. Ladislaus sort of beat it out of me. You see, you aren't supposed to draw or write with your left hand. It ruins the symmetry of the room. So you'll find the nuns hitting children on the knuckles with rulers, attempting to get them to write "normally" with their right hands.

After that I didn't do much drawing. Or really much art at all. You couldn't tell by my facebook and instagram lately, though.

And if you looked closely at the tiny smudges along the left hand side of the thicker lines, you can see where the ball of the hand laid down.

These were drawn with the left hand.

I tried my hand at a few.

But my left hand was just no longer responsive. Which led me to wonder if I was doing this in my sleep. Like what if the nuns just sent my left handed artistry down deep inside, to awaken at night, where I would be a left handed Picasso.

No, not Picasso, but better than what I could do when awake.

As time went on, the art became more elaborate, more surreal, more challenging, even. I certainly didn't mind taking credit. These were representations of beautiful girls, mostly nudes. Some were really powerful and erotic. It got to the point where I was really excited to wake up to a new "gift" sitting next to my computer on my desk- the same computer I would use to build vapid powerpoint presentations and stilted, long winded dissertations on marketing needs for tiresome companies determined to create just enough value in some community to extend their fiscal lives one more quarter without expending more than the minimal effort.

Sometimes I thought that described my life.

Until I went to sleep. That's when the lefty virtuoso would arise and create.

I had too much free time.

Last week, I had the bright idea to set up a camera and record my sleeping self, to test my hypothesis. Not to kill the goose who laid the golden egg but maybe to force him to reveal himself- the goose. What could it hurt?

And four days ago, I sat there, in front of my computer, and watched the video files. A version of me, slightly thinner, longer hair, without my facial hair, stepped into the camera range and slid a drawing on my desk. Then, I got chills as he looked directly into the camera...

And smiled.

And that's when the bodies started appearing.

# Who is Johnny Fractal?

It started as a con, as a way to get away with any crime, really

When a computer hacker, an experimental geneticist, a retired special forces mercenary, and a legal genius, working together, invented the greatest criminal mastermind of the twenty-first century.

They created Johnny Fractal.

They falsified computer records, created throwaway DNA samples, built elaborate fiscal backstories, leaked stories and rumors and more and together, hidden from the public eye, they invented a human being, one of the most successful and deadliest of criminals that had ever lived.

And then, some seven years ago, they met one last time at a diner and, together, created the story arc of that character's death. They killed Johnny Fractal. And walked away with billions of dollars each.

So how was he alive now, and killing them one by one?

Lida stood over the body of Mercer, slashed to pieces in his own living room. Strangely, despite her 20 year association with the man, she had never known his name until now. The four had referred to each other, always, in code. She was Montana. He was California. And California was dead.

He was a lawyer, an accountant, a criminal fiction fan. And it was his idea, originally, to get the four of them together.

To get unimaginably rich.

Lida didn't look up. She assumed they were placed above. She would hack into the system here and wipe all traces of her presence later. But she didn't want to risk the cameras catching her face.

She had long hated that she had one of those instantly identifiable faces. But she was cute, a shock of bright red hair over her stunning freckled sleek brown face. At first glance she often appeared to be an anime character. And, in all honesty, she dressed like one, she thought, in her long black coat.

Mercer was the second one. Klein, an award winning geneticist was found dead nearly one week ago today, his head nearly severed from his body. The violence felt like Fractal, at least the version that Lida had helped invent. The two men had literally nothing in common except for their participation in the creation of the imaginary criminal, besides their great wealth.

She knew how wealthy both men were. It mirrored her own wealth. The four of them had split the take from Fractal's misspent life of crime four ways.

Lida opened a small box she kept at her waist. It was a raspberry pi computer, small but very powerful. She touched a few buttons and followed the stairs to the roof. Without looking up, she greeted the older latin man, "Nevada"

"You know I hate this," He countered, face half in darkness.

"You don't need to. I just transferred all my money to you," Lida appeared calm.

He was confused, "Why would you do that?"

"I'm young. I'll make another fortune. I'll make two," Lida sounded confident.  Nevada stared at her, trying to read her face.

Did he need a partner?

# The Hungry Dead

Louis sat on the toilet seat and waited. He had frantically called everyone he knew, and there was really nothing else he could do. Momentarily, he wondered why he had never considered hiding a stash of those marshmallow cookies here in the bathroom.

In case he locked himself in.

He sighed and started to run scenarios in his head.

It was a very different world than it was last year. If he were going to start up a company right now, maybe a tiny refrigerator for the bathroom would be a useful product.

He felt his stomach rumble a little.

As a little backstory on this new world, about nine months ago, something fundamentally changed in the atmosphere. Louis had heard speculation that global climate change had worked its magic to melt some icebergs and release a long dormant virus into the air.

The air, for its part, FELT thicker, it seemed harder to move through. Although experts said that might be an illusion, brought on by the virus, which some magazines had dubbed Externus.

The experts said a lot of things.

And then, people began to see the real impact of the Externus virus, as the recent dead began to return to life.

Oh, not all of them. If the brain was damaged too severely, that was that. Or if the body had truly irreparable problems, they might remain dead, as well. But for 99% of the people who died in those first few months, they experienced a miraculous renewal.

They came back to life. And Louis was one of them.

He was in a car accident on his way home from work. His heart was damaged and he was declared dead on the scene by paramedics. Until he wasn't.

The revivals had been happening for a few months at this point and the Paramedics knew to drop off the newly undead at the local hospital where they would be reunited with their families. Louis stayed in bed at the hospital for three days, enduring tests and research until he finally returned home to be with Nica.

She was overwhelmed, but so happy he was ok.

The papers went on about zombies, but, in reality, the people who returned were the same as everyone else. With one exception.

It had become clear that the brains of the newly dead were susceptible to damage- damage that might, if sufficient, turn them into mindless eating machines, killing and consuming the people around them. And what could cause this kind of brain damage.

The most pervasive thing was hunger. If they got too hungry, if they were starving, the brain was impacted. Severe hunger

could damage the brain, Hunger, when not alleviated, would force these new dead to become revenants, zombies.

The room started to glow red and a chill ran through him. Louis felt a kind of calm wash over him as he thought about how he missed Nica. He couldn't wait until she got home and he could finally eat.

# The Undocumented Crowd

The first thing that Ryan noticed was the woman's hair.

It was yellowing, in streaks, falling haphazardly over her face. This mop of hair was traditionally how Ryan drew women. His friends had said he was going through his bedhead phase. Maybe it was a phase.

But the woman in the third row looked eerily familiar.

It's possible Ryan had been awake too long. He hadn't really realized the true meaning of the concept "One man show" until he was set building, producing, directing, and starring in one. And it was exhausting.

He had just started his run at the Logue theater and so far hadn't invited his friends. But this woman. He knew her.

He thought he might have painted her.

That night, Ryan went home and fell asleep nearly immediately. But, in the morning he found it. Behind two other pieces near the fridge, this was her, he was sure of it. Could he have seen this woman around and just sort of painted her. And then, coincidentally, she came to the show?

Ryan took the train back to the theater and tried to put it out of his mind.

That night, the woman wasn't there. He scanned the audience, realizing he had never really LOOKED at the audience before.

And there, in Row E, behind a larger woman, was a man with a wild tousled shock of black hair over a pinkish face. Ryan knew, immediately, that he had painted him.

He barely made it through the show that night, rushing home immediately after curtain.

And there, next the pantry, 4 pieces deep, leaning up against the wall, was the piece. It showed that exact same man from the audience. The expression on his face was identical.

Ryan couldn't be sure, but the collar of the man's shirt, in the painting, suggested he was even, possibly, wearing the same outfit.

There was no show the next night, Sunday, so Ryan began an experiment, In the cool light of day, this entire thing just seemed stupid. Last night, did he really think he was painting people who magically showed up later at his show, right from the canvas?

He had three canvases left, the black ones he loved, 16" by 24". He was willing to sacrifice them for this experiment. Three hours later, he had painted a person on each. The first was a cherry colored redhead with a facefull of freckles, the second a black woman with a pompous skein of hair rising upward. The third, a man, had simple thin lips and a wan smile.

The next night, he stared at the crowd. He made excuses during the show to step from the stage into it.

And he saw all three.

Ryan took a cab home that night and picked up the can of acetone from his storage area. He sprayed it across his work, watching as every face melted, dripping, waxlike, onto the wooden floor.

And the next show was a true exercise in horror.

# EVENTS

It's only after we consider an event in the past
that we ever really seem to understand how it began.

# The Big Switch

........................................................................................................

Before the Big Switch, if you asked a room full of people to name the single most important event in human history, you would have gotten a diverse range of answers.

People might talk about World War Two. Or the Black Plague. Or even current pandemics, if they were young enough.

You would hear stories of the Holocaust and the civil war, which, although horrific events that changed history in powerful meaningful ways, were insignificant in long term impact compared to the Big Switch.

In fact, most of the nations of the world had restarted their calendars to begin on that day, January 1st. In the year we now consider year one.

As I sit here, writing this essay, hoping it propels me into the college of my choice, I know my task here is not to explain the Big Switch, there are literally thousands of books that have worked to do that, but to express what it means to me, now, on the one hundred and fiftieth anniversary of the event.

First of all, no one I know personally was there. And the people impacted personally by it are all mostly dead. On last estimate, from what I understand, about fifty people still live from that period in history, all of which are so old that they can't possibly be expected to see many more years. My generation hopes to live to two hundred, on our most optimistic days. The fact that some of this generation lived to over one hundred and fifty is certainly impressive.

Especially given the strains of the time.

The funny thing about the Big Switch, in retrospect, is that the core question it posed was actually a popular party game question. It was routinely asked around the table over punch and a rousing game of cards against humanity. "What would you do if..." and then, depending on how intimate you were with the crowd in attendance, it would either escalate into a sexual conversation.

Or a political one

Or a social one.

But always a rowdy one. "What would you do if..."

But when the Big Switch actually happened, it changed everything. When I think how unexpected it was, I know it's hard for me to fathom, having lived afterward, in the wake of its possibility.

We live now in a time where we expect it to happen again. It molds and modifies everything we do. We think differently, act differently, we care and nurture differently. And this is the world I was born into, so I don't know any differently. I have lived my whole life with that sense, as a man, that I have a responsibility to the union of women across the planet. And I feel, from them, that same recognition. Every day.

But it never happened again. And no one was ever able to determine why or how every single man in the world permanently became, over the course of twenty four hours, a woman, and every woman a man.

# Generation

The UEF Jemison was the first generational ship ever launched from earth. Constructing it cost nearly an entire year's resources for the entire planet and nearly everyone on earth had watched, over the last nine months, on every kind of media device, as it was readied to send to the stars.

Most people were familiar with every room in this great ship, with books written that covered every stage of its short life.

The Jemison was the first ship in the United Earth Fleet, but, suddenly, overnight, that fleet had doubled in size when an exact replica of the ship in low orbit, descending from the night sky on that chilly February evening, a full six months before its own launch.

Well, not exactly.

It had taken some abuse. The hull was thick with dents and impressions from small impacts with objects in its path. This alternate version of the Jemison was scratched and darkened where the original was sleek and silver and smooth. There were pieces missing and new ones, built and replaced. It had engines to maneuver where none were in the original specifications. And it had a greenhouse, built into the outer hull, pointed topward the starlight feeding the oxygen rich plants, an idea that the UEF scientists found particularly enlightening.

But the most surprising thing the Jemison brought with it to earth was inside. The original complement of the ship was going to be thirty eight people, men and women who would operate it and potentially fill the new colonies with life once they arrived. These people were planning, right now, to leave the planet they loved forever, and to populate new versions of earth elsewhere.

But this ship carried two hundred and three people, the great great grandchildren of the original crew. And, although many of them carried the names and even, to some degree, the faces of the original crew, none had met them.

Before now.

Members of that crew, both current ones and these new crew members, who had presumably, as it was now understood, come from the future, mingled in the UEF hall, sharing stories, trying to determine what had happened.

How had this ship returned home after relatively experiencing over one hundred years of travel, to a time before it had even been launched. And what had happened to it in that time?

These questions were not academic as the Jemison was prepared for its launch window less than a month away. A team of scientists reviewed the data in private, for fear that the future might be changed in disastrous ways if the knowledge were to get out.

They concluded, after a week of study that it was imperative to life as we knew it that the Jemison launch on schedule.

The team was briefed.

The thirty eight crew members sat in their launch seats, reflecting, each of them, on how prepared they had been to meet the unknown, but how different it was to rocket off into the known.

# The Tape

...........................................................................................

The box for the tape sat on top of the pantry refrigerator for months afterward, left unfound by the legion of people who had passed through that giant penthouse since Jiillian had died.

There were no words on the box, just glossy images of Jillian, seemingly pulled directly from her act, from her 2 award winning sitcoms, from her multiple films. A retrospective of Jillian's life, on VHS tape, of all things, something she left behind, maybe.

But, when the police asked around, polling Jillian's friends and family, no one could remember the tape. Oh, they remembered tapes. VHS tapes. Many of them.

A swarm of them.

It seemed that Jillian had fallen in love with the format. None of her friends could say why. Or when her passion began. But everyone in her entourage had had the pleasure of sitting next to her and laughing along with the various video tapes, all shot from Jillian's perspective, of jokes and scenes, film plots and more. All of them new and exciting for everyone.

To be involved, seemingly, in the creative process. It was a rush.

Jillian would watch, sitting next to friends and family, taking notes sometimes as though she had never seen them. And each time, a different tape. This one with a glossy box cover of her stand up show.

That was before Netflix had put her on the road for her award winning show.

This one with a brilliant and hilarious image of "Stuff it, Margie," her critically acclaimed sitcom. With episodes and jokes no one had seen. At least not yet.

Always on VHS. Always with a brilliant cover. Always the only tape in sight. That's how focused Jillian was. She wasn't concerned with what had happened in the past.

Jillian was only concerned with the future.

A future she lived to see, one where she was widely known as one of the most profoundly influential voices in comedy who ever lived.

A future she worked so hard for, some might say in an obsessed way. And Jillian's career wasn't marred with missteps and false starts. When she did something, it worked. Her attention to the future had paid off.

Jillian's friends would say that they had never known anyone so fixated on the future. Her manager would say that was why she was so consistently good at what she did. And so committed to watching herself grow on tape.

That's why it was odd that a search of the house found no videotapes. No covers, Nothing. Just the one box on top of the fridge. With no tape to be found.

The police assumed that her friends had taken them as souvenirs of the beloved comic

The box itself eventually found itself in the evidence lockup of Police station 17, just a few blocks down from Jillian's place, unrecognizable to the Detectives that had left it there, its newly emergent cover a glossy and altogether unremarkable image splayed across the front darkly showing Jillian's overdose.

# What We Eat

The Recipe Expo was an event not to be missed - and not just because of the aliens.

The Talokians were small and cute and leathery green. It was always a huge surprise to people who were just encountering them that they didn't look altogether unlike Yoda. And they tended to be kind and soft spoken, so the resemblance really didn't end there.

And we had sort of inherited the Recipe Expo from them. It was a quarterly event on their world. People got together and created amazing meals, delicious foods, whose recipes would then be entered into the replicators.

These microwave-sized food printers were a gift from the Talokians. And soon they were all over. They were easy to build, once we saw how, and they made food directly out of materials found in the air. Overnight world hunger was essentially over.

And everyone on earth ate.

The Talokians considered eating a joyful event. And so they invented these Expos. Everyone all over the world would have access to these recipes. And the joy they brought

There must have been nearly ten thousand people at this one. They worked on recipes at home, refined them, played with them, but at the expo, it was sort of a virtual event. No additional groceries were needed. You input your ingredients and methods and the machines made them a reality.

As a sort of amateur chef, I admit I was pretty impressed. That was before, you know. But still,

Impressive.

It was an uncensored sort of event. I think a lot of people enjoyed that part of it. I mean, we censor food. Consider Foie Gras. In order to make it, you have to be unimaginably cruel to a goose. Many states have banned it. But there was no reason not to enjoy the virtual replicated version.

Bison, Panda, Cheetah, Komodo Dragon, there was a transgressive air to many of the recipes, almost as though people felt that their hands had been suddenly untied. There was no need to worry about how many polar bears were in the world when eating your polar bear stew or how many emperor penguins were left when the small plate penguin pastilles were trotted out.

The Talokians, in some ways, had liberated the palate from the prosaic every-day-ness of traditional cuisine. And that was, I think, the beginning of the problem.

Because, what would YOU DO? Right? Maybe you wouldn't create beautiful outrageous dishes with Barbequed Bald Eagle wings but at some point, you might get curious.

And this event certainly sparked the curiosity. With tens of thousands of chefs, at least one or two had to consider, "how would human meat really make this dish sing?"

Or maybe more than that. Out of ten thousand people, they knew that one percent might.

And that's enough.

After all, they were a very old race - old enough to understand what would happen, eventually, to any species that had, in some way or another, developed a taste for itself.

# The Convention

..................................................................................................................

"Why do we do this?" Albio asked, earnestly, a blue drink in his hand, "I literally get nothing out of this."

Rono knew the answer, "Because it's fun. We can live in the moment. That's got to be worth something."

Albio had to admit that he was having fun. "Do you want to have sex behind the silos?

"Sure," Rona pounded her fruit punch flavored drink. She could tell she was about to be plastered. She thought it might make sense to have some fun first. A short but eventful ten minutes later She was on her knees in front of him, finishing him off. It would have been fun if he could cum in her, but that seemed like kicking a stone down the road, she thought.

"Uh. I'm so glad we met." Albio felt strange being so vocal about that, but he was. He really wanted someone playful to spend the day with at this convention.

"Ok, but you get me off next. Maybe near the big machines." Rona buttoned up her pants and rose.

"Deal. I want to see those, too."

The two made their way to the chicken wing booth and pretended they hadn't planned that, each one. They had Teriyaki wings.

Rona asked first, "So what do you have going on here? " she fingered his temporal belt.

Albio looked proud, "oh, this is 24th century tech. It's minimal exclusion, between worlds stuff. It does time and dimension."

Rona was impressed. She had taken him for a 22nd century time merc. But she still had him beat.

"Check this out. The best that 2750 has to offer. It has intangible observation mode and quick time recovery protocols." she pointed to her harness, a sleek silver thing, wrapped in a playful fashionable leather.

Albio drooled over it, "Damn. You get sexier by the minute."

"Yeah, well, let me know when you're ready again to do something about it." She laughed. She honestly couldn't remember the last time she had this much fun.

It turns out Albio was willing to take that as a dare. He fucked her behind the big machines and once again in the time viewer. Rona started to feel like he might be the part of the day that really paid off the most. She leaned back against his arm during the "History of time travel" feature and tried to feel the closeness. She liked his lips. And if she had to admit it, even the magnificent temporal technology wasn't flooring her tonight.

But he was. This simple guy from three hundred years ago.

The night slipped away. Rona held Albio's hand a little tighter walking up to the Rotunda to exit. She gave him one last kiss and stepped into the snapback cylinder. She knew it was the only way but she hated it today. It was their job to protect the timestream.

The last memory of today to be wiped from her head was the feel of Albio's hands on her.

# The Workers in the Well

Today was the grand opening of the Well.

I know a lot of people object to alien technology, in general. Many of them are just conspiracy theorists. Some have reasonable concerns about elements in alien tch that don't conform too stringently to traditional physical laws.

And, yes, that I get.

On this project, however, the protesters outside had a completely separate horse to beat.

I'm not sure if that language is offensive now. Maybe it is to horses.

ButI honestly don't really know how to think about it. I mean, I dimly understand that I'm one of the reasons they're protesting. But you can't hardly blame that on me. Or on any of us, for that matter. We didn't ask them to protest.

Ok, I should probably explain.

The original designs for the Well came from the Ven. Originally we had seen the power of it when the earth was aligned, at certain times, with their well in orbit around their planet. It resurrected various people who had died, when it was in alignment, filling their bodies with the spirits of deceased Ven citizens. As you can probably imagine, this created some conflicts. These revitalized dead were named "Kintsugi" after a Japanese technique to fix broken pottery with gold, making it more beautiful.

The Ven approached us later that year, trying to help fix what they had, well, broken. They were the third alien race that citizens from Earth had met and by far the tallest.

So tall.

Soon after, work began on our own version of the Well. it would draw the essence of people who died here on Earth and safeguard them, so that they might be returned to bodies.

Usually their own, after some maintenance and reconstruction.

It was people like me who worked on the Well. Which is part of the problem, I suspect. I'm not exactly a skilled worker. Much of the work, internally, was just labor. Virtual and real. The inside of the device is effectively a virtual world, a meeting hall, a place where the dead can congregate and communicate, to effectively "live" until they are retrieved. We had much work to do on the outside of the machine, but also on the inside. Tens of thousands of hours of work. To prepare for this day, the final launch.

I'm not joining in with the protestors, for sure. But I do understand. And a part of me is really sympathetic. I appreciate that there are people in the world willing to stand up for me, for us. And, if this had been someone else in here, who knows?

I don't.

So, in reality, this protest here is really for us, the workers who built the inside of the well - those of us who had to be murdered every morning for years and brought back at the end of the day so we could finish the internal construction of a device that was here to make sure that no one ever really died again.

# Grounded

...............................................................................................

"This won't be the easiest press conference in my career, but I hope that all of you will be patient with me." The room erupted the second that Gabrielle entered through the stage right door. She wasn't sure anyone had heard her.

"People, I need you to keep it reasonable or we won't learn anything."

That, she thought, did not work, either. She tried a different tactic, "Shut the hell up!"

That actually did manage to calm the room enough for her to begin. She secretly gave thanks for her partner, who was admittedly, a bit rougher around the edges. It may have been rubbing off.

"At 2:15 Eastern this morning, The astronauts Michael Verenzano and Patricia Oakland disappeared when their ship attempted to exit the solar system. As you all probably know now, both of these astronauts reappeared here on Earth exactly seven minutes later, at 2:22 am Eastern time in their respective apartments. We have no additional information to provide as to what forces made this happen but NASA has every confidence that it will have some answers shortly. Now. Any questions?"

Every hand shot up. Gabriella Reese sighed and began the mental calculations in her head. Who would be easy on her? She took the enquirer first, hoping the story they seeded had paid off.

"What do you say to the accusations that this has happened multiple times before, at least four times, our information says, including the launch of the DIAZ?" a wild eyed woman in front began.

Thank you, God, thought Gabriella. "I know you are looking for your Bigfoot quota here, Ms. Grant, But we will send you the physical data of the entire trip of the DIAZ. It was entirely uneventful." Gabriella leaned back a bit, confident that this had done the job. In truth, this had only happened twice before, but hopefully this wild tale from the enquirer would help cover that up.

"Do you suspect alien involvement," started a grey bearded man in the third row.

She wrinkled her nose, "Honestly, Mr Stevens, we do not. What we have encountered here is likely a naturally occurring artifact of this universe we are working hard to explore right now. However, it has encouraged us to pull back on programs headed for deep space until we can determine their safety."

"And how long might that be?" a woman in back asked.

Gabriella lifted her blank notecards and pretended to read. "It could be up to eight to ten years.

The crowd grumbled and broke out in confusion.

The truth is that this was not what Gabriella had signed up for as press secretary. She hated lying to the press. She hated subterfuge. She hated all of it. But, at the end of the day, she would hate, more than anything, having to explain the terms of the alien treaty they had signed almost forty years ago that kept them on probation, grounded here in their solar system, for another ten years.

# The Eternity Plague

Shala released the torn and bloody fingernail covering his left middle finger. This left no nails on his left hand as he stared at it in the cool blue antiseptic light of the hospital bathroom. His eyes were wet and red and he let himself sink to the floor.

He was in a boardroom. He was at the head of the table, in a black suit and a purple tie, bored, waiting for the speaker to finish off her presentation playing on the glass wall next to him pitching a new kind of corn, one that was immune to pests and larger than previous efforts at bioengineered corn.

She flipped to the next slide and began to extol a set of virtues about the new marvel, starting with an item that piqued Shala's interest.

This corn was capable of lasting long periods of time on the stalk, unpicked, without aging, without rotting or becoming inedible. Shala urged his dream self to stand up and make his way toward the smaller asian woman. Iit took four steps to reach her. On the second, he grabbed a pen from the board room conference table that he used to stab her again and again in the throat, sending thick red webs of blood to the floor as the rest of the participants screamed and ran from the room.

He woke up in a pool of vomit, still in the hospital bathroom. He cleaned himself, as much as he could, and shuffled out into the hospital corridor.

He stumbled past other hospital residents, some impossibly old. The shambling skeleton in front of him looked like he might have been already prepared to die when the plague hit, some seventeen years ago.

Shala dug the remaining fingernails of his right hand into his forearm and felt the rush of pain. Since he was a child he was able to use the pain to travel in time, to fix things. And his body, crumbling and mutilated, was evidence of his efforts to do that now - to fix this plague. As the blood left his brain, he dropped to the ground.

And was in a pristine laboratory. He looked to his left and saw the hastily drawn letters on the wall heralding batch 47, and how it had kept the test chimpanzee group alive for days longer than the previous batch. He confidently strode across the room in his spotless lab coat and wrung the life out of the baby faced pinkish man in charge.

He woke up to a set of impossibly old eyes peering at him from above. The media had started to refer to them as the hyperaged. This man was missing an arm.

The attendants didn't seem to even bother anymore. He pulled himself upright at the nurses station. Looking down, he pulled the letter opener from its rest, digging it into his forearm, hopeful that after this trip he, along with the rest of these revenants, would finally be able to die.

# The Ghosts at the Feast

I worked for Zero Point publicity so I actually had an in-person ticket to this thing. Nobody really believes I saw what I saw, but I did. And even the people who believe it don't really want to look into what it means.

You likely watched it on Netflix, that big live show. It was beautiful - the first marriage between a human and a Ven, the alien race who had recently reached out to us. It was also a royal wedding, so when I tell you that all the stops were pulled out, I'm not fucking around,.

The Count Jean-Phillip was an actual heir to the throne of France. The throne was defunct now, since France was a constitutional oligarchy like every other country. Don't quote me on that.

I have a background in Xenoethnology, the study of different cultures. Lately that means alien cultures after meeting three of these cultures.

The Ven were unusual ones because they had conquered death, in a way, centuries ago. They used a special tool to gather up the psyches of the recently dead and then implanted them in new bodies. This was technology they were willingly sharing with us, so, as you can imagine, spirits were high for the wedding and they, as a group, were fairly welcome.

If you don't have Netflix plus, though, you may have missed the interior part of the ceremony. The Count and his new wife, a tall greenish tinged woman named Khria both were required to be nude. This was a pretty amazing opportunity for me. The Count was very proud of his millionaire workout body, but that's not where the attention was. Certainly not mine.

Khria was apparently anatomically incredibly similar to earth women. She was hairless everywhere and her vulva looked nearly identical except for the greenish hue. Her breasts looked similar as well.

I'm getting that part out of the way so you can focus on what is really important here.

She stepped up to the dais and three Ven men, also naked, stepped out. She walked up to each and slapped them. As she did, each one handed her something, in his hand, which she ate.

This was the fascinating part to me. I overheard that these were previous boyfriends and that it was their culture that she had to "repudiate" them publicly, in order to accept her new partner.

The men didn't look happy, but I wasn't skilled at reading the Venn.

Until I looked closely. On each, a small patch of skin on their penises was missing.

A piece about the same size as what they had given the bride.

Probably harmless.

But my training and instincts told me otherwise. You see, our rituals are usually watered down versions of past rituals, and we retain their meaning. Did this ritual mean that, at some point in the past, in order to marry, a woman would have to kill her previous partners and eat their manhoods?

And how long ago was that?

# All the Red-Haired Children of Scotland

There had been relative peace between Scotland and England for about three hundred years until it was ruined. By a rumor. The rumor itself was at least three hundred years old.But it had lost none of its potency.

During the time of Robert the Bruce, when Edward the second invaded Scotland, the story goes that a tall girl, thin, with red hair and a deep brogue somehow drove the English king insane, killing him at Berkeley Castle and then, turning to his cowering fourteen year old son, Edward the third, encouraged him on threat of death to sign the treaty that left Scotland under its own rule.

From that day on, the uneasy alliance between the two countries would stand. Scottish painters would paint this scene for centuries, while writers wrote about it and minstrels sang. The Scots had won their peace. Until The rumor.

In 1650, English Forces found, in Edinburg Castle, a woman who looked identical to the paintings of the red-haired woman, some painted over three hundred years ago. She was taken into English custody and the standard English hospitality was meted out. Which was usually sufficient to determine what manner of threat someone actually is.  But she would not die.

Oliver Cromwell was called and he personally oversaw her torture at the hands of trained professionals, men who could reduce anyone to jelly within the space of a few minutes. But her body seemed to resist every torture inflicted upon it. The death penalty she languished under was now centuries old, but it would have to wait longer.

And she had still not spoken.

Cromwell saw her for what she was. A patriot. And he knew exactly what to do with that.

He released a proclamation calling for the murder of every red-haired child in Scotland and Ireland, a brutal reprisal, but a symbolic one, ensuring that every grieving parent would know exactly who was to blame...

This red-haired terrorist and threat to England.

The orders were carried out immediately,. And, for their part, the Red-Haired children seemed to know about symbolism themselves. They all died without making a sound. They died in quiet, robbing the English soldiers of their cruel pleasures.

Each child died as quietly as the Red-Haired woman endured her own suffering. And their family and classmates made no sound, either.

Cromwell stood again, in front of her and told her about their destruction. He laughed at her perseverance.

The red-haired woman raised her head from beneath the chains and finally opened her mouth. She spoke one word:

"Listen"

And that's when it happened. That's when the sound of every child murdered, amplified and made millions of times louder, slammed through the castle, reducing Cromwell and his army to sludge, reverberating across the English countryside, killing everyone who heard it until it finally grew quiet some few miles past the home of Charles 1, the brown haired king of England, who lay headless now on the ground after his eardrums had shattered .

# TRAVELERS

Every traveler needs a starting point.
A point "A" to connect to "B" with their journey.

# The Rock of Time

....................................................................................

They say that once you invent a time travel machine, you should wait a week to use it. If no one comes back during that week to kill you, it's probably going to be ok.

It was statements like this that led Bonnie to wonder who makes that shit up. Although, in all honesty, she pretty much had to wait a week until school was over.

No one wants to be lost in the swirling eddies of time during finals week.

Still, it was comforting to see that week pass uneventfully without a stream of time travelers fro the distant future arriving to murder her in her admittedly less than unbroken sleep.

"So, thank you, timeline," she thought.

The idea behind the time machine was very simple. If you could use magnetic resonance to detach someone from the timeline, letting them slip back and forth, a double A battery would be sufficient to produce enough energy for the actual movement through the time stream.

This meant that the entire thing could be stored in a hand-held device as small as a stone that fit right in your hand.

And Bonnie, ever the overthinker, thought that was a perfect way to disguise the device.

Imagine something as simple as a stone, held in your hand, innocuous in any time period, seemingly without value or importance, certainly nothing that would be taken by a thief.

It could be held in the traveler's hand and kept secure by just making a fist.

This felt important.

Bonnie had, for years leading up to this invention, had dreams about being burned as a witch for her possession of some arcane and elaborate futuristic device in a more primitive time. Or having that device pilfered by 13th century pickpockets or 23rd century master thieves.

She needed something no one would look twice at. And for days, leading up to its first use, she carried it with her until it became second nature to hold the small gray weathered stone in her hand.

Her first trip was to see herself as a baby. Pressing the near imperceptible depression in the rock face, she made physical connection with the metal contact below, which was able to read the synaptic stream held in her head, cut the skeins that held her fast in time, and propel her to the appropriate time and place. She came to rest in the past with a gentle spin that caught her momentarily off guard.

Bonnie was pleased to see that her recollection was correct, though. She was an adorable baby.

"This surprised no one," Bonnie thought, as she decided to test the machine with a trip forward

She spun into existence in the far future, and instantly fell to the ground due to the uneven flooring. As her eyes adjusted to the poor light, she could see miles of nondescript gray rocks stretching out in front of her, peppering the ground across a broken world, drenched in darkness, hard under her open hands.

# The Caseworker

Marina had gotten used to the red behind her eyes over the last few months. At this point it was almost comforting.

It meant she had work to do.

She watched James from above on an app on her store-bought iphone, coupled with a simple, modern-era drone camera. Like all caseworkers, Marina hadn't brought anything with her from the future except her implanted retinex, aligned to the timeline of her client.

Every caseworker only had one client at a time.

And hers, today, was James.

James was beautiful. His hair was thick and nearly white from the sun. His face was eternally flush from running in circles in the yard, laughing. He was completely unlike any other client that Marina had ever had.

Robert, for example, was cold and unloved by his parents. His eyes were dark and unforgiving. Marina could see how easy it would be for him to purchase three guns on the internet, 12 years later, and murder 17 people.

That was his path, until his caseworker pinpointed the problem and had him moved to a loving home.

For all of Robert's darkness, his path wasn't hard to alter. It was like a stone in the road that lodged in his bike wheel, sending him off in another direction.

His life changed.

Marina adjusted the drone. It was working sluggishly and she wondered if she should just take it back. The blades whirred in a rhythm that sounded, in all honesty, a bit sickly. She sighed as she began to recall it.

She was getting almost nothing on James, anyway.

He seemed happy. Graceful, even. It didn't make any sense. Where Robert was a dark black stream, James was a raging rapids, white and clear. She tried to wrap her head around it.

Around the Idea that James would, in 8 years, murder 116 people at a school dance. That this beautiful boy would shoot girls in the face as they pleaded with him to please let them go.

Marina shuddered thinking about it. The light behind her eyes was still red, meaning that they were still on this timeline, the one where James commits those horrific acts.

She stood up and moved closer to the boy. She could almost hear him from here, even without the drone.

Her phone buzzed in her hand, but she ignored it, trying to place him in the massive park.

She was positive, for a second, that she heard his laugh when she felt her head spin through a crown of pain. The drone had fallen, returning to its control point, blades still engaged, as the tiny pieces of metal became entangled in her hair, at least one slicing through her jugular.

As she fell to the ground, she saw James moving toward her. The blood streaming from her neck caused him to slide as he fell next to her, trying to stop the red swirl.

And Marina closed her eyes, for the last time on a beautiful field of green.

# Egg

Emmy and Sean had found Egg in the woods right behind their home in Clarksville, digging him out from the wreckage of his ship. The ship was cold to the touch and about the size of a refrigerator, if you stretched it out a bit and smoothed it down,

Emmy could see her face in it.

They took Egg home and nursed him to health and promised him he would be okay. He looked up at them with his greenish white tinged eyes, deep set in leathery green skin under a silver jumpsuit and tried to smile.

He was grateful for the two children.

Now, to really understand everything that happened here, you have to remember that Emmy adored her brother. She idolized him. Sean was sixteen months older but he might as well have been twenty for all the adulation she gave him. As far as Emmy was concerned, Sean was always right, always good,

And always her big brother.

Egg recovered quickly and the kids soon took him out, in secret, of course, to show him the town. They dressed him up as a little old lady and held his hand across streets while he gazed and laughed at their alien world. Clarksville had always seemed tiny to them, until they saw it through his eyes.

Egg was always full of wonder. He was alive with the kind of joy that comes from traveling, learning, and experiencing. And the three of them soon became inseparable.

And when Sean first began to get sick, she would sneak Egg into the hospital to stay up all night with him and laugh. They watched funny movies, scary movies, ate pizza off the hospital bed, and dressed Egg up elaborately to hide his alien features from the orderlies. At that point, though, Emmy didn't even really care. Nursing Sean back to health was so much more important.

Until one day it wasn't an option. Emmy and Egg showed up at the hospital to see that they had shaved Sean's head. The sickness had advanced and the therapy made him sick, made him throw up, made his hair fall out in clumps.

Emmy's parents told her to prepare for the worst and say her goodbyes.

She was so young. How was she supposed to let go of the brother she had adored her whole life. Or stop being sad once he died. Or stop herself from believing the men in the black suits who told her that Egg had somehow made him sick. Egg sent one last message home,.

Later, Emmy struggled to use Egg's communication box with her fingers, shorter and thicker than the alien's. There were tears in her eyes as she told his family not to come, that everything was over and it was all lost.

Hundreds of miles away, the CIA doctors cut into his still living brain and removed it, his tiny body shuddering on the table before death, as Emmy finished her message and destroyed the machine.

# We Are Wind

In Diné Bizaad, the Navajo language, his name meant "graceful," "fair," or even, and this made Elu laugh, "beautiful."

It had been a long time since Elu was any of these things, he thought. Age had ripened him, carving deep wrinkles into his face and hands, each one representing, he hoped, some good he had done, some boon he had given, life saved, spirits lifted…

Hope delivered.

But he was not beautiful.  Oh, he was a powerful man, but that power had been held in potential, locked in amber, unused.

Until today.

Elu was a teacher. In reality he had no choice. When your people's lives are taken from them, their land, their children, their health, and then even their very history, you have no choice but to build heirship- to leave your lessons for the next generation. Elu was wise and knew that his children's children would not look like him. But they would carry his stories forward.

Like the wind.

For Navajo people, the wind, Nilch'i, was an important force. The word meant more than what we think of as simply the air, the movement, the weather. It was the wind that birthed humanity. It was the wind that cooled and made livable the Dinétah, the home of the Navajo. But before there was a world, there was the holy wind, nurturing, serving…

Creating.

The wind fanned the potential in the world, much like it fanned the small fire into a rolling inferno, or a tiny wave into powerful breakers, tiny pebbles into a massive rockslide. Everything truly began with the birth of the Niłch'i Diyin, the holy wind.

But the wind had a placid state. As the air around us, it served us with every breath we took in.

Elu had spent his life in that placid state. He was the inactive wind. He had tried to help everyone he could, be the air in their lungs as they succeeded. He had lived a good life. This world had taken everything from his people. But rather than despair, Elu had given it more.

But let me ask you a question.

What if you were powerful, like the wind. What if you had a secret power that could change the world forever? A power that no one else had. But, you could only use it once

Right before you died.

Would you use that power, Like Elu, as you exited this world you loved so much, despite everything it had done? Would you stand alone, like he did?

Elu spread his hands and felt the air move through him.

He let go, atom by atom, of the bonds that made him who he was and embraced the Nilch'i that had made them all. And with a knowing smile on his weathered face, he became the lifegiving and precious wind, cool and nurturing, spreading out to the four corners of the world unstoppably, past every barrier made by man, birthing heirs from the raw material in everyone it touched

# The One Gram War

Ria knew from a young age she was a mover, a kind of programmer proficient with the very first design level of the universe, location, capable of moving through space instantaneously. In fact, she could trace her lineage back to Marisol Alvirez, the programmer in the twentieth century who became the hero Purge.

Which was a bit ironic considering where she sat today.

Scientists understood programmers a little better now. At first it was thought that the people who were learning how to control the universe design level by design level were normal people who had taught themself something remarkable.

Research showed that the few programmers on earth were a different species from traditional humans. Homo Sapiens Auctorus, they were called. In science journals, or "Authors" or, more commonly, by their public name, "Programmers".   And Ria was a very good one.

But a very distrusting one.

You see, the scientific research we're discussing here was not gained without sacrifice. And, like always, it was the people who were different who sacrificed.

The government, scared of a part of the populace beyond control, had dissected a number of her people. They started with villains and convicts, like the super villain Bliss, famously removing his brain for study.

Then they moved on.

Weeks ago, if you had told Ria that she would come here today, on her own, to meet with government representatives, she would have laughed in your face.

But that was before Una was killed.

Una was her partner who had lived with her here in Victory City in a beautiful two thousand square foot A-frame walkup that was now a pile of boards and stones because of him.

And he was one of the greatest heroes who had ever lived. Descended from a great hero, his great grandmother, he had fought for the city for decades. Until, for reasons no one could determine, he changed, turned. He began to use his unstoppable abilities to destroy the lives of the very people he had protected. Somewhere in that smoldering wreckage that was their home, was Una's body, still, unrecovered.

She fingered the tiny paperclip in front of her. She had watched their video and drunk their coffee and taken their money and understood exactly what they wanted her to do. Ria thought it was funny that they were so afraid of her that not one of them would step into the room with her to explain their unworkable plan.

And it was unworkable.

They wanted her to move this paperclip into the frontal cortex of his brain, to kill the invulnerable man. But it wouldn't kill him. It would most likely destroy the social part of his brain, leaving him a super-powerful animal, roaming the skies, killing.

She moved the paperclip to her hotel room, a souvenir, as she silently removed his brain and sent it into the heart of the sun, killing him without needing to see him.

It was better they not know what she could really do.

# Explorers in the Fog

Fifty years ago, the various nations of the Earth got together to accept an offer they couldn't refuse. In exchange for seven pieces of technology, given to them by three different alien races, they would agree to not leave the solar system under their own power for a full fifty years.

There was a lot of debate behind closed doors. There was arguing and in-fighting behind closed doors. In fact, all of it happened behind closed doors because only the top most level of government officials, worldwide, would ever know about the treaty.

To everyone else, it would look like the greatest boon that mankind had ever been given. Technology that would return the dying to life and let them change bodies if needed. Boxes that could easily replicate food out of materials found in the air. Machines that would show you your heart's desire and ones that could transport small objects to any location in the world instantaneously. Even devices that could allow you to view other timelines. All of these would be available to people across the globe.

And all they had to give up was everything else. They just had to abandon their birthright to the stars for a few generations.

That's all.

These nations couldn't even risk telling the top scientists at their own space agencies. So the aliens told them they would place a device around the solar system that would return people who attempted to traverse it, to their homes, unharmed.

It was called the fog.

Various nations had sent out ships, the occupants of which would invariably end up at home, in their beds, once those ships crossed the line demarcating systems. And only the elite across the world knew why.

But today, that would end. Leaders of every nation met with the alien representatives in a spirit of joyful possibility.

Which did not last long.

The aliens arrived, sullen, distraught. This would not be a day of celebration, but it would be a day that no one in attendance would ever forget.

On the viewscreen everyone could see the travelers headed toward the Fog as they disappeared.

The tiny wizened Talokian stood next to his cohort, the lanky Ven princess who had married an earthman as they admitted their deception. They had no power to lift the fog. It was the harbinger of a brutal, passionate warrior race of aliens called the Villi, and, time after time, it heralded their intent to invade and destroy the system it covered.

That's when humanity learned that its allies in the universe were small, scared, easily cowed by threats from the race that had conquered and destroyed thousands of others, leaving these alone if they were willing to lie, to give their forces a fifty-year head start.

People of earth had thought for fifty years that these great traces they had befriended were leaders in the universe. But the true leaders of the universe were the Villi

And they were on their way here now.

# The Greatest Race

........................................................................................................

Years ago, Humans discovered the current, a great waterway that spread across the entire planet, below the ground. The current is now considered one of the great wonders of the modern world. And it's the home of the greatest race ever attempted by anyone, in known history.

The Great Current Waterway Race was held every year at about this time and drew every kind of people from all over. There were even rumors that an alien or two might participate, a Taolokian or Venn. Maybe even one of the secretive and elusive Tau Raza.

But likely not.

People from earth, however, arrived in droves. The prize this year, a clean ten million dollars, all taxes paid to the appropriate government, was offered up by the brand sponsor, three years running, Red Bull

It gives you wings. Buut, I guess, also fins.

So when Elizondo and Robert rented out the top-of-the-line submersible, it wasn't a bad investment. Their ship had a unique design that took on water in one chamber when it submerged, becoming a submarine.

But one with a luxury pool in the center.

Which was helpful. Robert was a child of the water. He preferred it, loving to languish for hours in the pool at home. He knew sailing, he knew hydrodynamics, he knew navigation and he knew the current.

Elizondo was happy to have him as his first mate. In all honesty, though, they were really more equals. And that would become more apparent through the twenty-one days of the race, beginning and ending in Venice, Italy and going through over two hundred touchpoints around the world before returning.

They prepared with near-religious devotion. They studied, they trained. They learned about the life in the Current. It's estimated that there are more species of life in one square mile of the current than in the entire above ground world. This would be a unique opportunity for Elizondo to do the two things he loved- to travel and to explore the wonders of marine biology.

He was a bit of a nerd like that. And it was really no surprise when they won.

After accounting for sunk costs, rentals, food, ropes and devices, radios, etc. the two partners were still left with what looked curiously close to ten million dollars. In truth, the costs were really negligible. It was the effort expended that brutalized the partners, each of which would need to sleep for nearly two weeks afterward to catch up. As well, they discovered that many of the interviews coming their way paid handsomely. Their team-up was big news, across the world, really the first of its kind.

In interviews, the big joke was that much of the money might be spent on shoes, but the two laughed it off. What people failed to realize was that while Elizondo's five million dollar prize would go a long way in his world, Five million dollars could change everything for everyone that Robert had ever known in the Octopus world.

# The Hidden People

..................................................................................................

There have been, in human history, eight great gifts from the aliens of the universe, given to us by four different species. The last, given unwillingly by a race called the Villi, was our freedom.

So, i roll my eyes at that.

Seven great gifts.

The last of these were the pulse shifters, given to us by Tau Raza, the primary inhabitants of a world called Elian and they were what I did my dissertation on.

My PhD attests to the fact that I likely know more than anyone on earth about Pulse shift transporting technology and on the Raza.

Which is frighteningly little.

First of all, in their language, the "Tau" is an article, so it's redundant to say "the Tau Raza," even though magazines and even scientific papers do it constantly.

Secondly, none of us really know how transporter technology works. At all. Not even a little bit. The devices were handed to us by Tau Raza and they function perfectly, for objects under about forty seven pounds. So, it's easy, energy economical, and safe to send your small dog across the world to a groomer in Singapore and then receive him an hour later, or to send packages, food, etc. It's even completely safe to transport small children, who are forty six pounds or less. But on anything bigger, the devices just stop working.

They never told us why when giving us the technology. All we know is that no matter what we build it into, it stops working after that point. And nothing over forty seven pounds will transport. Iit is a great mystery. One we place alongside an even, potentially greater mystery.

What happened to the Raza?

It's been nearly three years since we've seen them. And in that time, the earth has gone through a lot. New York City was renamed Victory City to commemorate rebuilding it after our victory over the Villi. We signed new treaties, built new wonders, and discovered remarkable things in the earth below us, all without any participation by the Raza.

And I think I know why.

So, hear me out.

In my studies, I attempted to pin down the core biology of Tau Raza. It was hard. It seems there is tremendous genetic diversity in their population. The recordings we had show so many shapes, sizes, colors. But if you read between the lines you see more.

Transporting, as a person, an adult, into an unmonitored, unsecured location is incredibly dangerous. I imagine it even FEELS dangerous. The Raza have a quirk in their genetic code called "the flowering/" It's what lets their genetic phenotype to sort of shift and adjust to environmental challenges.

Since the attack by the Xenophobic Villi, it's become clear that being different is one of the greatest challenges. So what if The Raza's individual bodies were triggered by the dangers of transporting, and their appearance began to shift and change to make them look.. well...

Like us.

And they never really went anywhere.

# Waiting In the Dark

.....................................................................................

Oresta was born a princess in the complete darkness. She would one day be queen of the Blackout dimension. Surrounded by subjects without eyes, her ability to perceive shapes made her impossibly unique, a superhero in her own right.

She loved the idea.

And every chance she had, she used it to act like a superhero. To help usher in peace between two groups who had fought in the dark for centuries. To help parents find sightless children that had wandered off. To help even farmers, in the dark dimension growing food in the living soil to increase their crops, by directing them to resources only she could see.

She was the impossible superhero of an entire people. So when the other superwoman arrived, she instantly felt a kinship, a connection.

Even with her limited vision could see she was in distress. The princess asked her what she was doing there. She told her that she had run away from her life because she was uncertain what it could be. Her father had used her, changed her, tortured her, and she wanted nothing more than to be free.

Oresta could see inside her, the tiny machines that made her work, changed her, enhanced her. They were powered by a reactor in her belly, with enough energy to keep her alive for millennia. She was incredibly powerful.

But she was lost.

She had charged the machines inside her one day and made the request that they take her from the world. She wanted to die. She wanted nothing more than to be in permanent unending darkness.

And so she was. But not the kind she was expecting.

Oresta fell in love with her almost immediately. Just as she herself was a princess of the blackout world, this woman, Ara Zodiac, was a princess, of sorts, of the daylight world. And there would be nothing more natural for them to be lovers.

So the wasted days spent in bed, huddled closely together, laughing on the floor, locked in love, these turned into months, and they turned into years.

Time passed differently in the blackout dimension. The eyes of time were blinded here, and years spent would sometimes be just minutes in the daylight world. So there was no rush.

They fell into their love.

And one day, when Ara wanted to know more, Oresta took her to see the priestesses.

They read her future and told her that she would do great things, remarkable things. She would be a hero and save the world. But she would also do terrible things. She would be a villain and endanger it, as well.

She would live for a very long time. She would love so many people, only to watch most of them wither and die. She would capture the hearts of people who would one day turn on her before eventually loving her again.

She would live.

She returned to the womb of her bed with Oresta and dreamed about being born again.

# The Etherdimension

......................................................................................................

The hero known as Octagon had lost his father when he was younger. This was before he built the suit that enhanced his birthright and allowed him to travel in the etherdimension at will. He sometimes used that negative space dimension to move villains in and out of, weapons, armor, etc.

He once saved an entire building by rescuing them all to the etherdimension and returning them afterward. Sure, the place was dangerous, full of the occasional monster or demon. But even more dangerous was the effect of it on people.

In the etherdimension, all pain is muted. Physical pain becomes a memory. The mental pain that comes from discontent and ennui disappears. And emotional pain, the pain of rejection, grief, loss, these all fade quickly into wan greyscale versions of themselves in a wash of blurred that color-soaked world.

This might sound wonderful, but too long a time there, in the etherdimension, creates a kind of coldness. You begin to detach - to no longer really feel. He had learned, as a boy, that his father was born there, in the distracted wastes of that dimension, cold, painless, and one day had escaped to earth to love, to feel everything he wanted to feel.

In his honor, Kasim would often take off his Octagon suit and volunteer at the local children's hospital. He spent time with children who were looking at hopeless conclusions to their too short lives. He felt for them, he felt with them. He brought them and their families food and toys and when there was nothing anyone else could do, he did what only Octagon could do.

And this, I think, is why he is always remembered as a real hero. Not because of that Rio hotel fire when he saved three hundred people. Or the endless battles with Cavera and the rest of the Culling where he ported them away before his insidious death vision could kill hundreds on the street. Or even the battle of Victory City where he helped save the whole world.

We want heroes who sometimes act more simply. Like we would.

As human beings.

And that was Kasim.

He was there nearly every day. He played with the kids. He fooled around. He told jokes. Today, he sat by Jill Nierman's bed and read her stories from a giant book on the bed stand he had brought. He took whatever time was needed to let her father Stephen rest and recharge.

He thought about how his father had disappeared back into that dimension when he was young. How he was pulled back against his will. Every moment counted.

So when Jill knew she had little time left, Kasim put on the suit and drew them into the etherdimension, where he sat watch as she laughed and enjoyed her last few days, with her father at her side, free of pain, free of regret, light in each other's arms as the glow slowly faded from her eyes, eventually dimming to nothing.

# ENDINGS

Even in a book of beginnings,
there is always a chapter full of endings

# The Lat Days of the Echelon

Uman sat hunched in his chair around the massive round table of the monitor room. For the last twenty years, this had been his seat, his home. It even had his symbol carved in the back of it. When he looked down, he could see the near-microscopic indentations bearing his fingerprints where his invulnerable hands gripped the handles at the side of it a little too hard, watching villains on the view screen.

It was comfortable. And today would be the last day he would sit here.

The triple row of photographs depicted some of the previous members of the Echelon, headshots, action shots, group photos, everywhere he looked, the ghosts of the super heroic world, some still alive on distant planets, like his grandmother, Ultra. Some, like Kingdom, Transverse, Muse, now just memories with aging biopics heralding their great wins and tragic endings.

One or two of the supers were still here, still active, still fighting evil over a hundred years later like Zebayon, Legacy, Apex...

There were one or two others.

Uman used to feel invigorated at the sight of this wall, empowered. He stood on the shoulders of these giants and he could feel their, well... energy in the room, I guess, for lack of a better word. But, now, today, he couldn't help but think that many of them were the problem.

The Echelon was not the first enterprise to close its doors because it was too effective. It had been months since any of the other members were here. A year or more since any founder had bothered to show up. And why should they?

Uman floated out to the deck, adjacent to the monitor room, and rose up to the roof. He looked at the world he had helped create.

No hunger or material want didn't stop crime immediately. But it had taken the wind from the sails, created a space where criminal henchmen and collaborators were impossible to find. And when the power hungry elites were removed from the picture and the laws were rendered more just, serving the people better, fewer and fewer of those people had found a reason to break it.

And now, today, without much fanfare, lacking purpose, he was silently putting away the memory of the Echelon, the greatest superhero team in the world. He, alone, had shown up to pack, to celebrate its end, to mourn, to say goodbye.

And he did. He let go and let the power inside him lift him.

From a few thousand feet in the air, Uman considered the long legacy of the Echelon and how it ended today with no one left to fight. He wondered sometimes if the existing membership even knew how to fight anymore. He was positive that they would never be able to stop someone, even just as powerful as himself. But they would try,. And that would be enough.

The twin arcs of his Laser vision rained down on the city, destroying the building he loved.

# The Final Battle of the Beetle

Stepping out of the pod on Kessler six was a different kind of lonely for a man like Verado who had experienced every other loneliness there was.

There was, for example, the loneliness that comes from standing, by yourself, a kid, watching the television deliver stories about your homeworld invaded, and seeing the face of the invaders, giant warlike beetles and feeling real fear inside.

There was the loneliness built by watching your father and uncle, mother and older sister, sent to fight and never return.

Or the loneliness made by watching each of your friends, one at a time, turn eighteen and leave to fight, to die.

And, finally, the kind of loneliness that moored you on your planet, in your home, keeping you from the fight, only because of an accident at birth that had stolen one leg and left a rounded nub at the top of your pants leg.

Loneliness had made Verado feel small, worthless. He lost nearly everyone he knew. And then had to watch as superheroes and leaders, celebrities, people he respected, all fell to the powerful, nearly random attacks by the Beetle horde.

Beetles were less technologically advanced, for sure, but they were twice the size of a man, covered all over in a dense, impenetrable carapace colored in swirls of red and purple like a bruise on its second day. They spit venom and were nearly impossible to kill. But humanity tried, They brought everything they could to the war.

Except Verado, who was left out of the fight.

So he put himself in it.

It was true that he wasn't a fighter. Even if he had had two working legs, he was thin, sickly, and physical exertion never seemed to build muscle on his hunched over frame, just pain, and awkwardness.

But Verado was a genius. One of the revelatory moments of the paper he would publish on his return was the fact that traveling in time AND space was actually easier than just traveling in time. The energy produced by moving a body backward in time turned out to be a multiple of the mass of the object, like his pod, for example, and a factor of e, the speed of light, increased by the amount of time diverted. This energy would have to be expended or the object would explode.

But before that happened, it could be used to create a warp effect that would allow the object to quantum tunnel anyplace you wanted - like the planet where the Beetle race originated. Millions of years in the past.

Looking down, he saw one, the tiny beetles from which the race emerged.

It clawed at Verado's artificial toe, its beautiful reddish-purple exoskeleton already thinning and losing its luster from the chemicals pumped into the air when the pod had first arrived from an embattled future. Its forelegs tried to gain a foothold on the boots of this giant intruder, unaware that it was fighting the final battle for its species.

# Free From Gravity

This is an historical document - a secret one. You're probably used to this by now. In this world there are secret histories everywhere. This one I leave behind to vindicate a hero and call out a villain.

As you probably guessed, I am the villain in this story.

But none of it started out that way. It started over seventy thousand years ago, when a great hero was born, a man who grew to realize that he would never die. He discovered, as well, that he was now forever free from gravity, a force he could control and warp to his will. He saved humanity from a great catastrophe and then went on to save them again.

And again.

He lived his life as a true hero, keeping the human race under his wing, protecting them, fighting always for what was right. For a time, like many of his kind, he was even a superhero. And this is how I met him.

I was sixteen years old, in short pants and a tiny domino mask, a sidekick fighting under the name "Prodigy," capable of learning anything. And I did. I learned how to be a hero at his side. And then, one day, I betrayed him and he never knew it.

Back then, we humans had met three alien species. We had some differences, but things were mostly friendly. They warned us about the upcoming Villi incursion, even providing us with a few captured members of this alien race so that we could learn from them. And I learned that we were not going to win.

Even with the advanced alien tech at our disposal and all the various superheroes across the globe, we had no chance. They were massive, violent, unstoppable, quick, organized, advanced, brutal killers. And there were millions of them.

When they arrived, however, they discovered that we had one card to play, against which they were helpless. This ageless superhero for whom I was the sidekick, had, only a few years earlier, encountered an alien race even more aggressive. Eventually he had no choice but to use his abilities, ones that had become more powerful every day he lived, to create a massive black hole that ate their entire galaxy, leaving nothing behind.

And the Villi had no counter to this. He was unkillable. And he could eliminate their entire race from the universe.

The hero renamed himself Omega. He was tortured with the memory of the trillion souls he had murdered, far more than the number of people he had saved in his long life. And they could see it in his mind.

They retreated.

And that is the legacy of my sin. That I was so afraid that we could never win the war against the telepathic Villi that I learned from them how to implant memories and put the memory of a trillion person holocaust in the mind of the greatest man I ever knew, knowing that his heart would be broken forever.

# The Red Line

..................................................................................................

When times were hard, she would sometimes think about how these facetimes with Anthony were the only things that kept her sane.

They were always close, even when he was a baby. She was five years old, the very first one to change his diaper, the first one to burp him, the first one he smiled at. In a lot of ways, Anthony was in her soul, his voice part of her brain waves. And not having him here, next to her, was so painful.

She did all the things she needed to do to make the connection work and signed on. For a second, the camera showed an empty room. Then, his face appeared, smiling ear to ear.

"Sissy." he yelled out.

"Hey Ant," she returned. I thought you weren't there for a second." she realized that she had been holding her breath and she let it all out with a slow, easy woosh..

"I'm always here for my Sissy." He responded. She could see him settling in the chair for a long talk. She knew he loved these times, too. She could just feel it. 'So, tell me about your day. Include gross kissing stuff but you can leave out math."

"Gross, Math. And I'm not kissing anyone. I can't let losers near these perfect unenhanced lips." Cerise made kissing noises close up into the phone screen. Her lips must have looked huge from the other side.

"Aaah," Anthony cried out, "I thought that was one of those giant supermodels destroying the city."

"Oh, my god,  The council of brunettes forced me to see that movie two days ago. Did you get it there? Obviously you did."

"We get all movies here." Anthony sounded like the Buddha when he talked like that. She let it go. He paused for a minute. Then asked, "Are you still doing it?"

"Well. Yeah. Obviously." Cerise felt embarrassed but also slightly annoyed. She never wanted to talk to Anthony about this. She didn't want to talk to anyone about this.

"Talking to you is important to me right now.," she admitted. She knew he felt bad. He dropped the point.

But he knew that Cerise had been cutting herself for years now. It wasn't something she could just stop, and not today. She looked down at the row of red slits up and down her arm. Toward the center was a new one, still oozing blood, a drop of which ran down the muscle to the floor.

One day she would stop, but she had discovered there was power in the blood. Power that let her do things other people couldn't. It was intoxicating, to experience that power, to know that the body could create an opening in possibility for people willing to challenge it.

But every night she vowed to stop.

The next day, however, she still slid the letter opener across her arm, releasing the blood, like she had done every night to call Anthony ever since he had died.

# And Every One a Window

Endy watched Garaki's art supply burn down, traveling all the way across town to catch the tail end of the fire. This was the end of an era, for sure.

When he had first found Garaki's thirty years ago, he was a poor student. He lived with seven other people in a sixth floor walkup with no elevator, so even carrying one of those canvasses up the stairs was a sacrifice. And every dollar spent on art meant less for food. Or shoes.

Or anything.

Through the years, though, each sacrifice paid off. He stood at the edge of the roped-off area in a Versace shirt. He wore two hundred dollar silk pants and shoes that cost...

Actually he wasn't even sure how much the shoes cost.

He was a wealthy man, but that was only a small part of it.

People who aren't artists forgot what life was like when Andy Warhol was alive. The world was electric. And everyone could agree, for that period of time - that short period of time, who the greatest artist in the world was. Until he died.

And the world never agreed again.

Endy wished he could stand alongside Warhol today. His paintings hung next to Warhol's in museums all over the world. He had the unique honor of having a piece in the MCA, the MOMA, the MET and the Louvre.

Even Warhol hadn't managed that.

And he owed so much of that success to Garaki's. The beautiful partner he had met on that art tour in Tel Aviv, his handsome Paulo. In a way, very realistically, he owed that relationship to Garaki's. The children that the two of them had raised, one an artist herself on the Sienne, and one, an actor in a wildly popular children's show.

Even all that, he owed the tiny art store.

He remembered trolling through the store, looking for the perfect colors, the right pens, refillable markers, acrylic paints that were vibrant enough to tell stories with.

But most of all he remembered the canvasses. Choosing a canvas was always an art form itself. The right size, the right shape, the right tooth, even the right color. He remembered the very first time he had found the right canvasses, stacked up in back, old, the wood they were stretched over yellowing and fading.

It was the older canvasses he found that worked.

And he would return, over and over, for one. Pulling aside the new ones to find just the right one. And, clutching his prize, he would make his way to the register and pay some small amount.

But never again.

Back home, Endy pulled out the last of the Canvasses he had from Garaki's, one of the black ones he loved so much. Experience told him that everything he painted here would come true, that it would happen in reality. As he planned the piece, he silently tried to figure out how to get every remaining wish he had into a single picture.

# Feeding the Garden of Justice

........................................................................................

Arisu knew it was her job to change the world. That's what she was born for.

She just didn't know the details. Until now.

Her home was beautiful, pastoral, a shinden-zukuri in Tsurui, Japan, a remote but beautiful area. She had chosen it for just that reason. In 1923, there was only one reason for anyone to travel to Tsurui and that was to kill Arisu. In her sleep, preferably, with futuristic technology, definitely.

She had built this home in the time it took a hummingbird to flap its wings once. And when she was done, the nails were warm beneath her feet, heated by the friction of a speed so intense it could only come as a gift of the eternal earth, mother of all things.

The world was changing and Arisu loved keeping up with it. She loved to learn and to grow. But the thing she loved more than anything was learning from the endless stream of assassins sent from alternate future timelines to kill her.

At first she found the information puzzling. She tried to make sense of it all. As time wore on, there was a picture painted, a picture of possibly future events, ones that she was destined to stop. The idea that she could be the lynchpin, the thing that created a better future for everyone, was so powerful that it lifted her from bed every morning, alive and prepared to fight.

And she did.

Every day, she confronted some new time traveling demon - monsters with the faces of men, looking to eviscerate her. And every day she captured them and learned from them. She interrogated them, hobbled them, then left them in her spacious garden to feed the cherry blossoms and abundant garden, grown from the evil of the men below, sanitizing it, as the earth did, and producing beauty.

She wrapped her fingers around the throat of this one today, listening to his final words, ones she had been waiting for. Names. Locations. Dates.

She moved at the speed of thought across Japan, his body in tow, and back home again.

Arisu used her speed to dig the hole, over ten feet deep, to prevent the local animals from catching the scent of the body, but prepared and buried the body at a normal human rate. She felt that this was a respectful approach to the process of burial.

But, as she laid this final monstrous traveler to rest, she found it hard to hide her excitement. After years of fielding these assassins from future timelines, she had managed to wring from them the knowledge she needed to end it once and for all.

She watched his body disappear behind the last of the dirt and ran this final information through her mind. The names she needed, the men these merchants of evil had tried to stop her from killing were in the same jail cell right now, in Landsberg prison in Southwest Bavaria.

Emil Maurice, Rudolph Hess, and Adolph Hitler.

# What the Hell Happened to Magic Loom

Katsu slid into the overstuffed chair and flicked through the remote. He turned to his left, excited, "Dude. There is a documentary on Hulu about Magic Loom. We have to see this."

The cranky voice beside him did now what it generally did best. It complained. "You know, we watch what you want to watch all the fucking time. Would it really wipe your ass that hard to hand me the clicker every once in a fucking while."

Katsu was willing to give as good as he took today. "Yes, it would, because all you want to watch is anime all day. And into the night. You see, we could both learn something from this."

"Learn my tidy brown asshole, bitch."

Katsu took this as ascent and flipped to Hulu. Magic loom was a corporation operating in the US for decades. At its height of market dominance, it had produced the costumes for most of the superheroes running around. And then, just as suddenly as it appeared, it disappeared when one of its invulnerable super suits failed, leaving its owner, a second tier superhero, dead on the ground, impaled.

It was a good story. Hell, even Katsu had gotten his suit from Magic Loom.

He was a mutant, born superhumanly fast. But, it seemed, just not fast enough. He called himself Tokyo Rush and wore a bright red and white pinstripe costume. You may have heard of him. He saved a school once. Not that it mattered. As fast as he was, he was no match for Vector, another Japanese super speedster.

As a Numina, she was about twenty times faster than he was.

And did she really need to be Japanese, too?

Katsu sighed. Still, he'd had some good times. Out loud he said, "Yep, we had some good times."

"Speak for yourself, Speedshit. I got shot a lot."

Katsu had to admit that was true. There was a lot of shooting.

But that was Magic Loom's selling point. Its costumes were often indestructible, bulletproof, and fireproof. Some could even prevent mental control. No one had any idea how.

Until now. The Hulu show went on to explain how Magic Loom employed a loom that actually was Magic. And it had come directly from Hell. Eventually it corrupted everyone who worked with it. The story was intense. And the graphics were good.

"Damn, these recreations are beautiful."

"Suck my dick, Tokyo Bitch. It's a fucking made for Hulu movie. It's not Endgame."

Katsu sighed. He felt his blood pressure rise. He wondered aloud how much of the show was true."

"It's as true as my dick. Wanna see?"

Tokyo Rush grabbed the red pinstripe costume from its resting place and placed it on the closet for the final time, feeling a wave of relief as he did. Looking at it reminded him of a time that he wanted to forget. And it was long past time to put all that nonsense away.

Besides, nobody talked to him like that.

# The Mushroom Cloud of Peace

There are these moments in history, times when the earth itself needs to intervene. In big ways…

and small ways.

If you are reading this journal, you are probably a friend of mine and you want to learn my story about the end of war. Or you are looking for brownie recipes. It's not really MY story but it's one I kickstarted.

The recipes, however, are mine. Make the mint ones, for sure.

It started, for me, with a Bob Marley record. Exodus is a perfect record, not gonna lie. Every song is perfect. And, as a whole, as a gestalt, it carries with it this feeling, this sort of ineffable truth. The entire record, listened to as a whole, makes you feel like we are all connected, all part of the same wheel somehow. And even though we might not like this spoke or understand that spoke very well, the wheel itself is real. And it is endless and inescapable.

You KNOW this feeling. You got it at your first high school sleepover when you sat there with your friends at night and everything went away except this feeling that we're all the same - that we're all connected by something.

So you heard the record, you like the record. Now let me introduce you to mushrooms.

If you and mushrooms have never met, you're welcome.

Mushrooms create that feeling. And they do it organically. There is a network that runs through the entire earth, this mycelial network. Mycelium are the hidden parts of mushrooms, the "roots" for mushrooms. They are many times longer than you think - kind of like the telephone wires of nature's communication network. Through this network, plants and trees work with fungi in a symbiotic relationship.

And us, too. If you reach far enough, you can see it. This network intentionally includes us.

And I feel included.

The mycelial network is a never ending game of red rover and you know what? We can all come over. No one is restricted. No one is too "bad" to be a part of the network. No one is too stupid or too hurtful or too perverse or too anything. We can all get in.

And here's what I'm really good at. We can massage the network and let other people in. From thousands of miles away. We can include old friends, enemies, boyfriends, girlfriends, rockstars. We can even reach out in this network and include people who run countries. We can pull in people with their fingers on buttons, people with red phones calling in air strikes. We can create a network that pulses with every heartbeat on earth, alive with every mind, too.

So, did i use this network, the one that travels through us all, everywhere on earth, to get a bunch of world leaders high as fuck so they would see what every 10th grade highschool girl sees as truth at her very first sleepover and put the bombs away?

I sure as fuck did.

# The Goodbye Machines

Erin was a familiar, a member of the race Homo Sapiens Affinitas. And she was having a wonderful last day.

And to people watching, if there had been any, it would have looked for all the world like the strangest and most wonderful of all Disney movies. Today, Erin did all the things she always wanted to do.

She woke up and made toast, swapping a few funny one-liners with the toaster. He, like everyone else today, made a pointed effort not to look sad but to enjoy life. She could tell that he was well-rehearsed and she imagined him whispering his jokes to himself in the middle of the night, gauging them for how much each would make her laugh, and making decisions as though he were a professional traveling comic. The thought made her smile even wider at him and burn her toast twice in a row, reveling in his company.

She rode up and down on the elevator, sharing her thoughts with him and listening to stories of other riders, people from her building, people she didn't know. He talked about Casey, the young girl from the garden apartment who would visit Erin from time to time. She knew she was a familiar, and even had a poster of her from her superhero days a million years ago. She knew she could bring machines to life and talk to them, and she secretly brought her watch to her to fix, now her inseparable best friend, clinging to her wrist as she waved across the lobby in the mornings.

After an hour or so of riding up and down, Erin sat in Celia, her autonomous car, feeling her gut threaten to leap out of her body in laughter at the car's witty sarcasms as she roasted pedestrians on the street to keep Erin entertained. Until she reached her destination.

The carnival was closed for repair, but the machines throughout the park spared no wonder, no effort, to give Erin the greatest day of her life.

She watched as the toy guns gave her a twenty one gun salute, the bumper cars lined up to ferry her anywhere, and the funnel cake machines conspired to create the most fantastic treats for her, waiting patiently for her to take a bite.

And when the rollercoaster, alive with the boundless energy brought on by fearlessness, let her down gently at the end of the track she knew it was time to go home.

As she closed her eyes for the last time, she remembered her husband, who had adored her every minute for over seventy five years, the light smell of his aluminum skin and oil that made her feel so at home, the living light in his blue diode eyes that she saw fade on his deathbed when he made her promise to have fun, to enjoy every minute she had left, to celebrate the life she had shared so openly, and to spend it in joy and with friends.

# Who We Are at the End

....................................................................................

There was a woman, at the end of time, who was very old.

She sat by the edge of a pool, algae collecting on the surface, in a wasted husk of a world under a reddish sun, speaking to her sister, who came and went, but was likely never there.

"Are you good today, my sister?" asked the infinite

The woman looked up at her. She knew that her sister's abilities had included traveling in time, but the Infinite one she knew had died hundreds of centuries ago. Everything in this world was now a sock on dead hands, trying to speak.

"Oh, I wish you were here." the woman eventually responded.

"Can I tell you a secret?" the sister, tattooed all over, still had the playful fire of youth, and it seemed so out of place here, the woman thought.

"Yes."

"I do, too. I'm happy to have moved on. But I never meant to abandon you."

The woman looked at her beautiful sister. "Go. I'll be fine."

It took nearly one hundred years for her image to fade from the sticky amniotic air. The stink of ozone threatened to kill the woman and that made her laugh. She had been born a few times and had still not yet died. The way it worked was that she would get stronger with the passing of time.

And she could feel that she was so much stronger than when she had gone to sleep, millenia earlier.

She leaned back on her feet  and watched the pool simmer and sputter. She cleared away a small branch from in front of the tiny creature slinking through the mud to the dry land only a few feet away.

She watched as it moved.

She had tried to be a hero, once. And then, failing that, tried to be a villain. Then, once she had lived enough, turned her attention back to being a hero. But these moments, thousands of years long, were still like shoes she would try on to walk around the store.

These stories all seemed to belong to someone other than her.

She righted the small creature who managed to flip over white navigating a tiny hill. He was brave. But he was stupid, she thought.

A combination shared by everyone she had ever loved.

She thought about her other brothers and sisters. She thought about teammates and lovers and people she had saved and people she had killed. She thought about pain and about how every part of the body can be used to make you feel good.

She gave up, tens of thousands of years ago when she let herself sleep. When she woke up she wondered. Had all of them failed to save man or was man destined to just die on his own?

And wouldn't it be funny if she lived for this long just to now become the captive savior of these tiny creatures. She righted her tiny charge again.

She didn't return to sleep.

THE END

ORIGIN STORIES FROM NEW EARTH

www.ingramcontent.com/pod-product-compliance
Lightning Source LLC
Chambersburg PA
CBHW051340020726
47501CB00007B/2181